Tl

Priyamvada N. Purushotham was born in Chennai and has
lived in many Indian cities. She has worked as a copywriter
at Ogilvy and Mather and taught French and theatre at the
Alliance Française de Madras. She now lives in Boston,
Massachusetts. This is her first novel.

The Purple Line

PRIYAMVADA N. PURUSHOTHAM

HarperCollins *Publishers* India
a joint venture with

New Delhi

First published in India in 2012 by
HarperCollins *Publishers* India
a joint venture with
The India Today Group

ISBN: 978-93-5029-138-2

2 4 6 8 10 9 7 5 3 1

Priyamvada N. Purushotham asserts the moral right to be identified
as the author of this book.

This is a work of fiction and all characters and incidents described in this
book are the product of the author's imagination. Any resemblance to actual
persons, living or dead, is entirely coincidental.

HarperCollins *Publishers*
A-53, Sector 57, NOIDA, Uttar Pradesh – 201301, India
77-85 Fulham Palace Road, London W6 8JB, United Kingdom
Hazelton Lanes, 55 Avenue Road, Suite 2900, Toronto, Ontario M5R 3L2
and 1995 Markham Road, Scarborough, Ontario M1B 5M8, Canada
25 Ryde Road, Pymble, Sydney, NSW 2073, Australia
31 View Road, Glenfield, Auckland 10, New Zealand
10 East 53rd Street, New York NY 10022, USA

Typeset in 10.5/14 Berthold Baskerville
Jojy Philip New Delhi 110 015

Printed and bound at
Thomson Press (India) Ltd.

For my grandmother,
Rukmani

On ne naît pas femme: on le devient.
Simone de Beauvoir

One is not born a woman: one becomes one.

One for sorrow,
Two for joy

0

While the universe came into being with a big bang when an infinitesimally tiny concentration of something exploded and created matter, space and time in a split second, I plopped into this world after twenty-four hours of arduous labour.

That's what mum said.

'You didn't even cry, you whimpered. We had to hold you upside down and spank you on your bottom.'

I was born in the sixties. When flower children were hallucinating on a sugar cube on the other side of the world and cellophane flowers of yellow and green towered over John Lennon's head, when Andy Warhol was exploding the plastic inevitable and Jim Morrison was lamenting the death of his cock, mum gave birth to me on a steamy July afternoon in Madras.

'There was a power cut,' mum said. 'Out of blood and sweat, I pushed you out of my belly, but when I saw your face the pain went.'

The pain went and I arrived.

Grandfather was an ophthalmologist. He came to see his thirteenth grandchild with an ophthalmoscope to establish the health of her developing retina. If I could read, he would have pointed me towards a Snellen chart and asked me to read the alphabet through the bars of my cradle. For the anaemic mother of the newborn, he brought an antidote tucked inside a newspaper bag, to thicken her blood and redden her colourless cheeks: two bottles of ruby-red wine.

Mum hated wine. My uncle guzzled it graciously and grandfather patted her on the back the next day and gave her another bottle. This went on for a few weeks when we stayed in grandfather's house. Everybody was delighted with my birth: grandfather, my uncle, mum. But it was grandmother who cried when we left.

Dad came to pick us up in his red Herald convertible with the top down. While my sister jumped into the back like a baby kangaroo, dad stuffed our overloaded suitcases in the dickey and then we drove away, my sister frantically waving goodbye to a tearful grandmother and grandfather, a cheerful uncle and aunt, and little cousins who ran behind the car as if it were a giant cricket ball. We were leaving grandfather's house in Royapettah for our home in Mylapore, one-and-a-half kilometres away.

Mylapore smells of frankincense, jasmine and dessicated piss. When you walk along Nageshwararao Park, you have to hold your breath a good sixty seconds and then release it when you're in front of the Amrutanjan factory where vapours of camphor and eucalyptus take over the clouds of urine. And for a moment, you think the promises on the bright yellow jar are true to their words: *For immediate relief from sprain, lumbago, cough, cold, headache and other complaints.*

I was a sick child. I had the flu every month and stayed up all night coughing. One day while taking a cycle rickshaw with mum to see the child specialist near the tank, we crossed the fringes of Kapali Thotam, the slum where the Mylapore maids lived. Suddenly mum became animated and pointed to the dark, pretty women walking down the tapering street. Their faces were stained with turmeric, their saris were all the colours of the rainbow and their anklets jingled to a slum dweller's beat. Mum said, 'Look how healthy they are. They have no money but look how healthy they are, and how happy!' I coughed like an asthmatic cat and nodded my tiny head.

I was a happy, unhealthy child who grew up between doctor's visits. While my sister played hopscotch on the pavement with the neighbourhood children, I sat by the window, propped my arms against the intricate grills and gazed at the pivotal squares.

My sole outings were when grandmother took me to the Music Academy to watch a play. Sitting there in the dark, air-conditioned hall, her silk shawl covering both of us, popping masala peanuts into my mouth, I forgot about my pathetic little life, my skinny limbs and congested chest. I fell in love with the people on the stage. I knew when someone changed costumes. I knew when the same actor played a different role. And most of all, I knew about the little home with the sofa set and staircase that led to a bedroom at the back. I knew there was no bedroom there. It was just an illusion.

One pale insignificant morning, a few weeks before I was to start school, mum decided to change my name from Malini to Mrinalini. She had been curiously examining a Sanskrit dictionary that she had found in the old steel trunk on which she kept photo frames over a crocheted doily.

'Aiaiyyo!' she cried and we all jumped from our chairs around the dining table. 'Did you know that Malini means gardener?'

I was discreetly blowing my nose into the checked tablecloth. My sister Maya was reciting her tables. Dad was reading the newspaper while expertly dipping his idli in hot sambar and popping it into his mouth before it broke into two.

When mum was pregnant with my older sister, dad chanced upon an abridged version of the Upanishads and came to believe that the real world was an illusion in the mind of the observer. When my sister was born, he perceived her tiny frame through his newly enlightened eyes and aptly named her Maya. When mum was pregnant with me, he was into cricket. If we have a son, he said to mum, I have a dozen names for him. But when I finally made my way into the world without a little dingaling, mum looked at me frazzled and baffled, and made a decision on the spot. Malini, she said to dad, catching her breath between syllables; rhymes with Kamini. And so I was given my first name to rhyme with mum's.

'A gardener! I can't have people call my daughter a gardener!' mum exclaimed. 'From now on she will be called Mrinalini. It means an assembly of lotuses.'

Dad looked up from his paper for a brief second and nodded. Fives ones are five, five twos are ten, five threes are fifteen, Maya recited at a feverish pitch. I put my thumb into my mouth and polished it off while nobody noticed.

And so the decision was made, simply one morning over undercooked idlis and a Sanskrit dictionary, to change my name. Since they called me Malu at home, I promptly forgot my new name on the first day of school. When the teacher asked me what my name was I told her it was Malini. She consulted her register and looked at me quizzically. Then I corrected myself and said Mahalini. She scrutinized it. 'No, I mean Sonalini,' I said. Then I tried everything from Shalini to Badrakalini and suddenly all the children who were wailing for their mothers a moment ago morphed into laughing Buddhas, rolling on their porcelain bellies and laughing their heads off. I laughed too. That's when the teacher threw me out of class.

'Twinkle, twinkle, little star, how I wonder what you are, up above the world so high, like a diamond in the sky,' twenty-five three-year-olds sang out of tune while I stood in the corridor blinking at them. Twenty-five sets of bewildered eyes were focused on me, so naturally I thought *I* was the star they were singing about.

A few years went by and I was standing in the corridor again. This time I got sent out for making a nude pencil sketch of Goddess Saraswati in my science notebook. This time I liked the corridor. The year was 1977. Emergency ended in India. *Star Wars* opened in theatres across the world. Orlando Bloom was born. Charlie Chaplin died. Josie and the Pussycats turned seven. And I turned eleven.

I still remember turning eleven. I turned into a butterfly. In the morning I was a fuzzy caterpillar trudging forward on diminutive feet, by evening I was a tropical butterfly with purple wings and scarlet veins. The sun looked like a mandarin orange and it was the best day of my life. I got my period that day.

I always thought that the day I got my period I would become a bona fide girl like Maya and all the pretty girls in senior school who were big enough to act as real women in the school play. Mum fussed over Maya on those days of the month. She laid out her uniform and packed her schoolbag, discreetly shoving sanitary napkins into compartments, while I threw my books into mine and dashed to the gate. It was only when I was backing my bicycle out of the portico that mum paid any attention to me. 'Don't ride fast,' she would scream as she ran after me. 'It's okay if you're late!' By then I would be halfway down the street, pedalling my bicycle like a pipe organ, tears streaming down my face.

But now I had it too! As the blood gushed out and my stomach cramped, the Madras sun turned from bright orange to deep red and I thought the sun was bleeding too.

'Look at the sky,' I said to Maya and reached for her hand.

We stood in the balcony, our heads above the railing, our hearts above a thousand flowers, looking at the blood red sky. Suddenly I felt a bond with the sun and the stars that were invisible in daylight. I felt a bond with Maya and all the girls in the world. I also felt like god because Maya pointed out that I now had the power to create new life. But mostly I felt relieved because I could miss PT class if I wanted to. I just had to tell the teacher it was 'that time of the month' and she would smile and welcome me to a secret club for girls only.

At home, mum circled the date of my first period on a calendar teeming with gods. There it lay: the number five circled with a marker pen, along with her date and Maya's, popping out with the eyes of Lord Shiva. She did this every month like an astronomer charting the collision course of the Milky Way and told me I had to keep track of the date.

'Why?' I asked.

'Because one day you'll see a pattern.'

Soon mum got a new calendar for the new year with

pictures of garden flowers. As the pages in the calendar turned and wild daisies became blue pansies, my body turned into a woman's. I was not a sick child any more. Puberty had entered my body and transformed it, turning every cell into a blooming unit of life, and with the rising levels of oestrogen, my vagina became thicker and paler pink, and my hips widened with my mind. And all the while the universe was expanding ever so slowly and galaxies were moving away from each other like red spots on a blue balloon that is slowly being blown up.

I was sixteen years old. I was five-feet-four inches tall and a 34 B. Finally I was part of the school play which had a professional director from a theatre troupe in Madras. The play was *The Glass Menagerie*. I was the stage manager. I worked on the costumes for all the characters, I prompted their lines, I sat behind the lights and came up with musical scores for the scenes. And on the evening of the dress rehearsal when the girl who played Laura was running a temperature, the director asked me to fill in for her. I donned her clothes and stepped onstage.

The next ninety minutes were a blur. I remember sitting in a circle of light in the midst of utter darkness, looking at a glass unicorn and feeling completely alone After the dress rehearsal, when I was sitting inside the green room removing my makeup in front of the mirror, the director came up to me and said, 'When you were looking at the unicorn, you were in solitude in public. You were living your role, Mrinal. Nobody has played Laura like this before and nobody ever will.' Tears filled my eyes and mingled with the eyeliner and dripped in large grey drops down my cheeks.

The next morning, I walked into the kitchen and told mum I wanted to be an actor. She stopped chopping beans.

'Let's see how well you play the role of a housewife!' she said and thrust the knife into my hands. I don't blame mum. She had had it with me. I often walked into the kitchen making preposterous announcements like that.

I went to the American Library and read all the works of Tennessee Williams. I mooned about the school laboratory studying poetry instead of chemistry. But when it was time to cram for my mid-term exams, it was as if my brain was divided in two – one half was crying out for literature, the other half for science.

A few months went by and I dissected my first frog in zoology class. I placed it on its back and pinned down its legs, cutting feverishly through the muscles to open up the body cavity. I spotted its heart, lungs, oesophagus, stomach, intestine, spleen, gall bladder, liver and when I saw its ovaries floating in the water like wings, I felt like Frankenstein on the day he chose to study natural philosophy. I'm going to be a doctor, I said to myself with great conviction – a doctor who will bring babies into the world.

I wanted to speak to grandmother because she had given birth to more babies than anyone else I knew. I bicycled after school to grandmother's house in Royapettah, pedalling hard against the northeast monsoon wind. I was the dot on the expanding balloon, drifting away from other dots, from houses and rickshaws, parks and seesaws, and people and people.

I sat with grandmother on the broken lovers' bench under the mango tree. Her face was like parchment and her hair was white and soft. She looked at me with one eye. Her other eye had been removed years ago after an erroneous cataract operation (ironically, grandfather had asked another ophthalmologist to operate lest he get emotionally involved during the surgery and make a blunder) and there was a glass eye in its place, grey in colour and completely unlike her soft brown eye. I was used to the glassy grey eye that always looked in the same direction. Grandmother had had it since the day I was born. But if you saw her then, with two incongruous eyes, each pointing in a different direction, you would never have believed how beautiful people said she was before the operation.

'Patti,' I asked, holding a wrinkled hand that was once full of flesh, 'why did you have so many babies?'

'Is that why you rushed here after school, you silly girl?' she said, laughing.

One of grandmother's legs was affected with elephantiasis and it was swollen like a balloon. The other leg looked tiny in comparison. Just like a hyena's, I thought. A hyena's front legs are longer than its back legs and its heart twice the size of an adult lion's heart, giving the hyena the stamina to stalk its prey at great speeds and end a chase at thirty miles an hour. Grandmother's heart was twice the size of anyone's heart. When I came home from my first day of school with tears streaming down my face, she was in our house in Mylapore, waiting for me at the gate. She lifted me in the air, wiped my tears with her spindly hands and put her soft pink lips against mine. That was my first kiss.

Women are nothing like hyenas. Female hyenas are larger than the males. They have more muscle mass and are far more aggressive. Their vulva is fused to look like a scrotum and testes. Their clitoris is so large that it looks like a penis and their vagina runs through it. They make love through the pseudo penis that stretches wide open to allow the male penis to enter while mating, giving the female complete sexual dominion over the male.

Indeed, women are nothing like hyenas.

'I don't know why,' grandmother said finally. 'Women just had babies those days. Your great-grandmother had seventeen, from the time she was fourteen to the time she was forty-five.'

I was looking at the mangoes in the tree. They were fleshy and bursting with juice. Like her hand, I thought, like grandmother's hand a thousand years ago.

Then her eye lit up and she said, 'But these days women have a choice. They can have babies if they want and not have them if they don't want and if they find out they're pregnant when they don't want a baby, they can go to a doctor and pull it out. These days women have freedom.'

We sat looking at the clouds that made wallflower patterns on the sky. I was thinking of Sundays when I was little. We would come to grandmother's house and as soon as she saw me she would lift me up like a colourful beach ball. We would draw squares on the red oxide floor and play daaya kattam with long golden dice that clinked on the floor. At night she would feed me curd rice on the terrace and tell me stories from the Mahabharata.

My favourite was the account of Draupadi's swayamvara, how Arjuna entered the arena like a beam of light, shot five quick arrows into the eye of the rotating fish and won the ravishing princess with dishevelled hair. When he took her home, his mother unassumingly asked all her strapping young boys to share the prize among them and the obedient sons were all set to marry Draupadi, but her father, King Draupada, hesitated to give his daughter away. At that moment Vyasa, the inventive sage who wrote the epic, appeared and told him that this was her destiny. In her last birth, Draupadi lost her husband shortly after she was married and the heartbroken young widow prayed to Shiva to grant her a husband, but when Shiva appeared before her, she did not see him because her eyes were closed. I want a husband. I want a husband. I want a husband. I want a husband. I want a husband, she repeated five times. And so Lord Shiva granted her five husbands in her next birth.

Mum would catch me standing in a corner with my eyes shut tight, repeating: I want a new dress. I want a new dress. I want a new dress. I want a new dress. I want a new dress. Or, I want a baby brother. I want a baby brother. I want a baby brother. And she would smack my bottom and say, 'How many times do I have to tell you that's just a story?'

'Oh, really,' I would retort. 'Then why do you have a picture of Lord Shiva in your bedroom?'

I looked at grandmother. She was still looking at the sky. What was *her* story, I wondered, this woman who gave birth to a string of babies when all she wanted was to learn to read and look at the sky while she still had two eyes to see with.

That's when I realized that a gynaecologist's real work was not to bring babies into the world. It was as much about the termination of pregnancy as it was about the culmination of it. If I could give women the option when they needed it, what a liberating experience that would be.

The sky had turned dark grey. It looked like it was going to rain. I kissed grandmother goodnight and sat on my bicycle. This time as I pedalled, the wind was in my direction. I reached home and parked my bicycle in the portico. I could smell dinner in the kitchen. It smelt like fresh earth. I knocked and Maya opened the door. When I stepped into the house, it started to rain.

———

Something opened up inside me that evening in grandmother's house and I stayed up most of the night watching the rain from the window. When I finally went to bed, I slept like a baby, curled into a bundle under the sky-blue blanket that was taken out of the attic on rainy nights when it got chilly. Maya slept beside me, underneath the same blueness, her long legs drawn up and wrapped in her arms. I lay under the warm blue expanse, sleeping dreamlessly for the first time in my life. Since I was a little girl I had been plagued with nightmares. When I was six, grandmother gave me a silver talisman suspended on a thick black thread. 'This will soothe nocturnal depressions and dispel nightmares,' she said and tied it around my neck. Whether it dispelled nightmares or not, the grotesque silver amulet certainly kept other children at arm's length. My aunt who lived in America got me a red willow dreamcatcher to hang over my bed. 'Bad dreams will be caught in the net,' she explained. 'Only good dreams will filter through.' But somehow good dreams never filtered through and bad dreams slamdunked into the net and landed in my head. 'The people in your dreams represent different parts of yourself,' dad said to me time and again. 'Try and understand them.' I tried very hard, scrutinizing different parts of my body, but I never understood.

But from that night on, I slept dreamlessly. When I woke up, it had stopped raining; the sun was back in the Madras sky and arched across the great azure blanket was a perfectly symmetrical rainbow beaming at me like an inverted smile. I dashed out of my room and went looking for mum and dad. They were sitting at the dining table, sipping their morning dose of filter coffee. I marched in and announced that I wanted to study medicine. Dad looked up from his shiny stainless steel tumbler and smiled. That was the first time I had spoken of studies.

If you are born into a Tamil Brahmin family, studies come before anything else. You learn to recite prayers to Saraswati – the goddess of knowledge who sits dextrously on an oversized lotus with four hands – as soon as you start to talk. When you are six you are taught Carnatic music and if you just can't carry a tune like me, you are made to sit cross-legged and play a veena twice your size. While boys play cricket and girls play the veena and both play the fool together, whether you are a boy or a girl, you have to be interested in studies.

Dad was looking at me proudly.

'I told you she'll come around,' he said to mum but she wasn't convinced.

'This is her latest fad,' she told dad without looking at me. 'Every two months, it's something different. Last month she wanted to be a zookeeper!'

Mum wasn't too far from the truth. While Maya was studying computer science at Anna University and got a *centum in maks* like a good Brahmin girl, I was having a whale of a time and sustaining my marks in the eighties.

But now everything changed. Afterschool volleyball sessions lost their charm. Phone conversations with friends dwindled. My textbooks acquired a phosphorescent glow and I spent all afternoon in front of the window with a science book spread across my compliant lap.

I breezed through my board exams. I topped my class. I got into the All India Institute of Medical Sciences in New Delhi. I boarded the Grand Trunk Express with a trunk full

of dreams and came back five years later with an MBBS and
a Punjabi boyfriend.

Maya married her classmate from college and they moved
to the Silicon Valley. My Punjabi boyfriend didn't last long
because his mother wanted him to marry a robust Punjabi
girl who would serve him tea in bed. So he was replaced with
a shiny Syrian Christian who took me to San Thome church
in his open Gypsy. I stood inside the cool Gothic structure
that smelt of the sea and prayed this would last for ever and
ever, until I thought I heard the voice of Saint Thomas from
the tomb. I quickly changed my mind and decided that what
I needed was a non-believer who had balls.

That's when Sid came along in his apple-green slacks
with long hair and a short attention span. I always had a
thing for boys with short attention spans. It provoked me to
find a way to keep them absorbed with what I was saying for
longer than five seconds.

I met him at a poetry reading at the British Council. He
was sitting at the back, and during the question-answer
session he asked the poet something about Madras. I turned
my head to look at him and I knew instantly that he wasn't
from here. His eyes looked as if he was pulling her leg and
yet he wasn't, that was just the way he looked. I realized this
later when he came up to me and asked me if I was a poet
too. I laughed and said, 'At heart.' Then he asked me what
I did and I asked him to guess. He tried everything from
pianist to psychoanalyst, enumerating all the things that I
had told my mother when I was a little girl. Then he threw
his arms up in the air and gave up. 'Gynaecologist,' I said
and he arched his eyebrows. 'I'm doing my residency,' I
said and he looked at me as if that explained everything.

Sid was a travel writer. He had biked from Kashmir to

Kanyakumari. He spoke six Indian languages. ⌐⌐⌐
spoke to me for the first time, something dissolved inside
me like salt into water and the sea ran through my veins
instead of blood. I did a day and night shift at the General
Hospital for thirty-six hours at a stretch and then walked
into his arms. When you stay awake for so long, night
merges into day, darkness into light; grill patterns take on
a new meaning and clouds speak to you in startling shapes.
Daylight falls on your face like lace and your senses become
so heightened that when you make love, you can feel every
shift in his body, every quiver, every spasm; you can feel
every stir and ripple that it sends down yours and you want
to scream because you are about to fall off the earth and
enter an altered state of consciousness.

You would think that I had found my prince, but unlike
the princess lying on layer upon layer of downy mattress, I
had not found the pea. If I had, we could have put it in a
glass case and marvelled at it, but then I wouldn't be telling
this story.

My man was a wanderer. I suppose I could have wandered
off with him and been a doctor without borders but I had my
borders clearly marked. I wanted to practise in this country,
within the invisible walls of this city. I wanted to work with
the women waiting at the bus stop, buying jasmine flowers
on the street and chomping on peanuts at the beach.

When he finished his assignment for the *Lonely Planet* in
Madras and moved to Calcutta on another assignment, I
thought it was over between us but I was wrong. It went on
for years. The night before he left, when we were both sitting
on his terrace with a bottle of Red Riband vodka, whooping
it up like there was no tomorrow, an airplane twinkled past
above our heads and he asked me to pack my bags and

come with him. I laughed and told him he was asking me because he knew I couldn't leave.

But I did leave. I finished my one-year internship at the General Hospital and left for London to specialize in gynaecology and obstetrics.

—

A black Ambassador with a sunny yellow roof was waiting outside our house. Dad loaded my suitcases and mum looked like she had lost a limb and I squeezed into the back between the two of them. As the taxi drove on in a series of staccato sounds, mum recited a recipe for rasam and the city whizzed past in technicolour.

After doing my Master's degree at King's College and training under the illustrious Dr Ian Murdoch at Wellington Hospital, after turning down the numerous boys mum tried to set me up with, I came back to Madras in the brand new millennium, alone and eager to set up a gynaecological clinic in Mylapore.

As my plane touched down at Meenambakkam airport on the night of January 1, 2000 and the sticky sour smell of Madras entered my nostalgic nostrils, a hundred and fifty-five hostages of the hijacked Indian Airlines aircraft returned home from Kandahar to freedom and the new millennium.

I ambled to the prepaid taxi counter, juggling two suitcases and a duffel bag. What must it be like to be back in the arms of your loved ones, I wondered, after a week of not knowing if you would ever see them again? Was I doing the right thing, returning to Madras after all these years when my parents had moved to California to help raise Maya's kids?

It felt odd to come back home and not have dad receive me. I thought of all the times he had stood waiting at the railway station – my single-minded, double-chinned father in Terry Cotton pants – when I came back from Delhi on the Grand Trunk Express. He would crouch over the steering wheel and listen with his eyes glued to the road as I talked incessantly and grumbled that I had to say the same stories all over again to mum.

I looked out of the car window. A little girl with a powdered face and yellow ribbons in her hair waited with her father at the bus stop. A five-year-old boy held onto his mother for dear life as she rode a Kinetic Honda at full throttle. Suddenly I realized that there were no cycle rickshaws. The roads looked cleaner, the street signs were brighter. People looked smaller in bigger cars. In fact, the people looked so tiny I could block them out with the palm of my hand. When I sank into the backseat with my hand over my face, about to regret coming back, the gummy Madras air lifted me up with its familiar scent and I was happy to be home.

And so, as the world rolled into Y2K without a hitch, with planes still aloft and computers still running, and people eager to write three well-rounded zeros after a two, I set up a gynaecological clinic in Mylapore and moved into my ancestral home one furlong away, as dad would say. I painted the house and sowed new seeds. I removed his nameplate from the compound wall. *Dr Mrinalini Krishnamoorthy*, it now said inside a golden rectangle that glistened in the sun. *MD. OB/GYN*.

1

The scene opens in a consultation room – a large room with a high ceiling and bare white walls. To the left is a blue flush door that swings into the room and to the right is a bookshelf stacked with files. I am the narrator and, like Tom in *The Glass Menagerie*, also a character. Sometimes I play an important role but mostly I observe the characters around me and convey their plight to the audience. I sit behind an enormous teakwood desk and, like the absent father in Williams's play, there is Sid sitting on my desk, grinning from ear to ear. I look at the photograph from time to time but the spectators see only the back of a gilded frame. The room is lit by a large window with translucent yellow curtains. In the background is a tamarind tree with squirrels and in the foreground the characters come into the light one after the other and take a seat.

The first character to make an appearance is Zubeida. Zubeida, I am told, means essence in Arabic, like a drop of the vanilla you add to custard, and this Zubeida was the essence of all that womanhood is supposed to be. Patient and nurturing, she could cook, feed the children and read a book all at once. She could make love just like a woman but she was a little girl. Well, not so little. Like many beautiful things, Zubeida came in a big package that was well hidden.

When she walked into the consultation room for the first time, it was May. I remember because the newspaper said it was the hottest day in Chennai in a hundred years. Certainly not the kind of day you want to spend lying on the beach tanning your bottom. There wasn't an animal on the streets. I wondered where the stray dogs had gone. On the tamarind tree outside my window, there were no squirrels that day. They had packed their nuts and gone on vacation while the rest of us inched closer towards the sun and the sea vaporized into the sky.

That's when she walked in, trailing behind a small, older woman, and smelling like a Himalayan musk deer. She was wearing an enormous black burqa that roofed her seventy-five kilos. I could only see the tips of her fingers and her kohl-rimmed eyes but when she lifted her black veil I saw her cherubic cheeks and I realized she was very young. I also realized she was pregnant.

She is twenty, the woman said in Tamil with a pronounced Urdu accent. I asked her if it was her first pregnancy and she shook her head. She has two boys, the woman said. She has a lovely smile, I thought, a big voluminous smile that would always be hidden under a veil.

Zubeida didn't speak to me those days but the following year, when she came by herself, she spoke. It was like sitting in a corner alone and listening to the shehnai. You didn't know whether to laugh or to cry.

Tulsi entered on cue with her terribly attractive husband Dhruv in tow. When I glanced at them in the reception earlier, it seemed as if they were waiting in the wings of a stage. She looked nervous; he, reckless. He was holding her hands and whispering into her ears. Sitting in the loveseat in the centre of the bright waiting lounge, they were oblivious to the dozens of patients staring at them. People neither hold hands in public around here nor do they huddle over the crossword.

It was only when they walked into my room that I realized they were trying to stay in that one moment of time called passion, a moment that had already been breathed away in a street café. They reminded me of a love story I had read years ago, set in Paris in the autumn. I could imagine her leaning against a historic stone wall while his beautiful brazen head leaned over hers in an infinite kiss. All she had to do to lose that kiss was open her eyes and look at the leaves falling down. But she didn't lose that kiss, not that day. She held onto it with her eyes shut tight.

But that was a long time ago. Over the years, the passion had misplaced its dimensions, time had slipped away and the die had shrunk to a single point. And now they were in my consultation room trying to make a baby out of thin air.

She was an art director in an advertising agency. He was a freelance copywriter. She drew seashells in borders and bluebells in corners. He wrote songs in the morning and ads in the evening.

'We've been trying to have a baby for three years now,' she said.

'We've tried every position,' he said with a twinkle in his eyes.

She had a pageboy cut. His shaggy brown hair was in a ponytail. She was petite, he was tall. She was pretty, he looked like a reincarnation of a sixties rock star. She jogged every morning, she said. He woke up late, he said. I'll make you pretty babies one day, she must have said to him many moons ago – if you make love to me. And how they must have made love, again and again with a slim layer of latex to stop a million sperms from entering her body, until her fragile little egg went into a shell.

Now they were trying to break it open with a corkscrew.

———

When Leela walked in, in a straight line with perfect little steps, and seated herself delicately on the chair in front of me, I thought of the infinity theory: if a horde of monkeys were to jam away on typewriters for centuries, somewhere on a paper someday, a monkey will type out a Shakespearean sonnet by pure chance. She was the sonnet.

She sat next to her mother like an unblemished peach. It was a pristine morning in July. On my desk was a gathering of chrysanthemums popping their colourful heads out of a crystal vase; one yellow flower jutted out and drooped over her file as if it were searching for something. The light from the window fell on the vase and reflected on her face and lit up her hands. Her right hand rested on her left wrist and her left arm was on the arm of the chair. Her fingernails were neatly clipped and a diamond shone on her ring finger. She had a tiny dot on her forehead, small enough to symbolize vermilion and yet not big enough to be spotted at first glance. She looked at me directly and there was something unsettling about her oblique gaze. She had a coy smile, an ever so gentle curving of the lip that made you unsure whether she was smiling or not.

How I spurned that smile when I was younger. When I was in college, experimenting with life and falling in love and picking myself up like pieces of broken china, girls like her never did anything wrong. And all along they had that smile, that dispassionate turn of the lower lip that said all was right with the world. But nothing was right with the world; it was all topsy-turvy and I was trying hard to hold onto the handrails.

Her period was two weeks late, she said, and stiffened a little. Her mother nodded. I gave her a pregnancy test and read the results.

It was positive.

Her mother was exultant. Leela took a deep breath and her lips finally curved into a proper smile. One would have thought she was jubilant but I was sceptical of that seamless smile.

Leela was a computer programmer. While she designed, tested, debugged and maintained a source code of computer programs, life had made a different plan for her. She had a three-year-old boy and now she would have a girl, I thought imprudently, and everything would be perfect. When she left, I looked at the chrysanthemums on my desk. The yellow flower had descended and was now sitting with the other flowers, the oranges, pinks and yellows in unerring harmony. With a sleight of hand, Leela had rearranged them and now they looked perfect.

———

Pooja looked like a Babushka doll.

She was cylindrically curvaceous, the top of her head

rounded and her body tapered towards her feet. I imagined a set of identical nesting dolls of decreasing sizes placed one inside the other within her. She was sixteen. Her striking face dominated her body and a look of despair was painted on it like a rose on a desolate landscape.

And what had the sweet little teen doll done to deserve this? She had fallen in love without a parachute. She had been floating through the sky suspended from a hot-air balloon with only her volatile teen spirit for combustion and then the balloon suddenly burst open and sent her headlong into the ground.

When she walked into my consultation room in her school uniform with a heavy bag of books on her shoulders, she seemed to be carrying the weight of all the books in the world. She had done a terrible thing, she said, and now she was left with a baby in her stomach. I told her making love wasn't such a terrible thing. Her eyes welled up and she told me her story. It was like listening to Tchaikovsky's *Romeo and Juliet.*

I told her about contraception. Perhaps she should wait till she was older, I suggested. Then I told her it wasn't a baby yet, it wasn't anything like a baby and we would just be removing some blood. I think she smiled for the first time in days. I could see a whole set of nesting dolls smiling one after the other after the other inside her.

—

Megha was skinny. The purple and green georgette sari and the vermilion mark on her forehead accentuated her anaemic face. Her stomach protruded through layers of georgette and the purple stripes looked like arches. She wore a diamond stud on the left side of her nose and large diamond earrings drooped from her bony ears.

She came with a gigantic older woman who was dressed just like her. She waddled into the room like a demon duck of doom weighing a few hundred kilos.

'She is having girl,' said the thunderbird in a Marwari accent. 'She have to have boy.'

I looked at Megha. She was as pale as a heroine in a black-and-white film. I checked her hands to see how anaemic she was. Her fingers looked like they could squeeze a tamarind dry. Her ingrown fingernails were stained yellow and the lines on her palms revealed a woman who stood by the kitchen window all day spinning chapattis like spider silk. I wondered what she held inside her bulging belly and I wished for her sake that they were the emerging fingers and toes of a boy.

———

Anjolie trotted in elegantly, wearing a short orange kurta over a red khadi skirt. Her long layered hair fell over her shoulders like a mane and she looked like the technicolour lion in the MGM logo. When she spoke, her eyes lit up and breathed life into the motionless consultation room and instantly everything was transformed into celluloid.

She was a performance artist. A performance artist in Chennai is like a fish out of water. I was a fish out of water too. That cool evening in December when the sky was purple and the leaves were blue and the sun had melted into the distance, she walked into my consultation room for the first time. And the moment she walked in, it felt as if the sea had receded and waves were engulfing the city and there was water everywhere, and I was swimming, swimming to stay in that one moment of time when I could finally take a deep breath.

2

The nurse placed her file on the table and her name leapt out of the plastic cover in big bold letters. ZUBEIDA ZAINUDDIN. Age: 21. Past Obstetric History: Three deliveries of three healthy male babies. No complications before, during or after labour.

It had been almost a year since I first saw her. The nurse opened the door and I caught sight of her twinkling eyes, gushing with hope. She had always come with her mother-in-law but now she was alone, looking like an ominous crow.

One for sorrow. Two for joy.

'I'm pregnant again,' she said, 'and this time it has to be a girl.'

I had opened my mouth to say something but my jaw was glued to my mouth with an invisible layer of Araldite. I had barely heard her speak until now and here she was standing in front of me and speaking in perfect English.

'Sit down and tell me what happened,' I said when my jaw finally moved. 'It's hot outside. You can take off your burqa if you like.'

She began to remove the burqa. It was like watching the curtain rise before a play. The curtain was rising, inch by inch, and I could see the stage, the set, the head of an actor who just a moment ago was headless...

'Ammi died when I was born,' her story began.

———

I lived with abba and daadi. My cousins lived next door. We played hide-and-seek in the evenings. When the moon came out, we all came in and sat around daadi who fed us from a gigantic bowl. We would all wait to have the last mouthful because we wanted to be the last one to kiss those fingers for the day. I got to kiss them a second time because daadi lived with us. She slept with me. I always thought she loved me the most because I didn't have a mother like the others. It was only when I grew older that I realized my mother died while giving birth to me. Sometimes I felt sad about that, but then there was school.

I loved going to school. There were little stones on the sand outside our class and we squirted water from our water bottles onto the sand and believed they would turn into stones the next day. And the next day, there would be more stones. We would squirt more water and the day after that, there would be even more stones.

We were learning to count.

Math was splendid, but it was English that took my breath away. The stories in our English reader got more intriguing every year. I still remember the story about the model millionaire. I remember the story about the boy who ate seventeen oranges with the pips and peels. I remember the boy who fought with me in class.

The boy you fought with the most was the boy you liked

the most. I fought all the time with a boy called Sandeep Bharadwaj. We raced each other to the playground. We competed with each other to finish sums. Once, he put a plastic lizard inside my desk and when I opened it, I screamed. I pretended to be angry but I knew he had chosen my desk because he liked me the most.

I loved physics and chemistry. I loved history and geography. We learnt about the Silk Road and the Spice Route. We learnt to draw the map of India and fill every state in a different colour. I always coloured Tamil Nadu brown because then it looked like the silhouette of a curly-haired boy with Pondicherry for its eyes.

I loved every class except the needlework class that abba sent me to down the road. I usually made something for daadi there. I gave her a left woollen sock, an embroidered handkerchief with my initials on it, and a blue wire bag. She never used the blue wire bag because she never went out.

At bedtime, I would sing all the songs I had learnt in school to daadi. I would tell her about the laws of motion and gravitation. I would tell her about the theory of magnetism. I would tell her about Sandeep Bharadwaj. By then she would be half asleep, murmuring, 'I'm still listening to you, Zoo, just finish all your stories today!'

Life was beautiful.

And then I got my period.

When a Muslim girl gets her first period, she must start covering her hair and body. I was worried that if I went to school it would be quite obvious to everyone who had seen me in two braids the day before. As it was, I was embarrassed about getting my period. But as it turned out, that was the least of my concerns. The next day, when I was getting ready, abba asked me where I was going.

'To school, of course,' I said as I tied my shoelaces.

'You won't be going to school any more,' he said.

I couldn't believe my ears. Why was he telling me not to go to school? We had a physics test that day and I knew I would beat Sandeep at it.

Daadi was ill and bedridden. How I wished ammi were still alive. I was too scared to argue with abba. From that day on, I didn't go to school. As far as my classmates were concerned, I could have fallen off the earth and landed in a black hole.

A few weeks later, daadi died. I wept for daadi, ammi and for all the women before me. But mostly I wept for myself. Then it came back: the blood. I hated it. I hated the colour. I hated the smell. I wanted to vomit every time I saw it but it kept coming. I wanted to find out the meaning of all this. While my father was away at work, I went to his room and pulled out the *Sahih al-Bukhari*. I went straight to the Book of Menses. I read it several times but found no answers. I remember reading this.

> *Um Salama:*
>
> *While I was lying with the Prophet under a single woollen sheet, I got the menses. I slipped away and put on the clothes for menses.*
>
> *'Have you got Nifas?' he asked.*
>
> *'Yes,' I said.*
>
> *Then he called me and made me lie with him under the same sheet.*

I wondered what it would be like to lie with Sandeep under the same sheet. He would kiss me goodnight and I would hold him and fall sleep. But that was all a pipe dream. I would never see him again. I would be married off to a thirty-year-old merchant at the age of fifteen. I would bear his sons. We would live in a two-bedroom apartment with his mother and brothers. I would be the hand that rocks the cradle, the breast that feeds the babies and the vagina that makes it all happen.

I would be nothing at all.

'Nothing at all,' she said in a small voice, looking straight into my eyes.

I wanted to take her in my arms and comfort her but I sat unmoving in my swivel chair. Say something, a voice inside my head said, do something! Isn't this why you chose this profession, to help women make choices?

But what choice did Zubeida have?

'I want to have a girl,' she said. 'I want to have a girl and be the mother I never had.'

'You are three months pregnant and you know as well as I do that there's absolutely no way to ensure that.'

Of course there were urban legends like having sex upside down under a full moon or in an igloo in Antarctica. Some people believed that more boys were conceived after heat waves and more girls after cold snaps. But if that were really true, whether there were dogs on the street or cats on the walls, there would be no girls in this sweltering city.

'We'll do everything we can for you to have a healthy baby,' I said, 'and we'll hope it's a girl.'

She looked at me and smiled that voluminous smile of hers. It was dashing, almost bombastic. It was an oxymoron like the bright pink salwar-kameez that she was wearing beneath the burqa. After noting the date of her last period, I did an internal exam. It always surprised me how she never quivered at the touch of my hand inside her. She lay still, looking placidly into the white, expressionless ceiling. Under the thick black veil, under the bright pink salwar-kameez, under the loneliness trapped inside the white cotton bra, was a woman balancing on a tightrope. Maybe she didn't have choices but she knew what she wanted, or what best she could possibly have.

After she left, I looked out of my window through the tamarind tree. It was very hot outside but there were squirrels on the tree. There were boys playing cricket. I saw her walking past the boys, past the flower-sellers and auto-rickshaw drivers, until all I could see was a speck of black on the street.

———

Tulsi burst into the room like a firecracker in October. She placed her pelvic scan on the table and looked at it suspiciously. Her eyes followed my hands as I took the scan out of the big brown envelope and held it against the light.

'Did I ovulate today?' she asked me as if she were asking an invisible man in the kitchen: Did I put salt in your eggs? Did I add sugar to your coffee? Did I step on your toes while dancing?

I had the awkward feeling that I was stepping on her toes. I was reading her pelvis like a map of the world unfolded and laid out on the table, but there was nothing I could do about it. She ovulated at the right times, her uterus was the perfect size, her cervical mucus was neither acidic nor alkaline. It was clear and stringy and good enough to eat. Dhruv's semen analysis was just what the doctor ordered: Grade A spermatozoa displaying rapid progressive motility, covering a distance of over twenty millimetres per second and exploding with natural lipids and essential amino acids.

But she couldn't conceive. I told her to let go, to let the world slip away and make love for the love of it but she couldn't. She had lost the Great Orgasm Debate. And now here she was, asking me if she ovulated. She would ask me again on day twelve, thirteen, fourteen, fifteen, sixteen, then hold her breath and count till thirty and start all over again.

'Did I ovulate today?' she asked again, her big brown eyes beseeching me to say yes.

Yes, I wanted to scream till my voice could be heard on the moon. Yes. Three little letters that make one big word. Will you dance with me? Yes. Will you marry me? Yes. Will you cheat on me? Yes. Yes. Yes.

She looked like Fantomina, the young lady of distinguished birth, beauty, wit and spirit, who sat in a box at the playhouse one night and saw all these men entertaining a woman who was making a sale of herself. How she wanted to be that woman instead of who she was.

Tulsi wanted to be the woman who would melt into her husband's arms like a cube of ice inside a microwave; ten seconds and she would melt into water, twenty seconds and she would evaporate into thin air.

That's how it was when we met, she told me. Everybody had disappeared behind the moon that night and there were only he and she. She was at his bachelor pad. There was a party going on somewhere in the background and people were drinking beer and talking. It seemed as if they were a thousand light years away and all she could see was him, across the room, playing his guitar and singing: 'Love me two times, I'm goin' away... Love me two times, girl, one for tomorrow and one just for today.'

He was leaving the advertising agency she had joined. This was his goodbye party to everyone. To her it was hello. The next thing she knew, they were sitting on top of the water tank under the overgrown moon; his shaggy brown hair was blowing in the wind and she laughed until the early morning sunlight was reflected in his eyes. They kissed. When she opened her eyes again, she could see the sunrise, she could see the water tank, she could see the empty beer bottles on the terrace; she could see everything again but it was all going round.

That was seven years ago. Now they were measuring their love by the tubes of toothpaste they had consumed together. She looked out of the window at the tamarind leaves. I looked at her short brown hair and thought again of Fantomina. Fantomina fell in love with a man who loved to sleep with many women. He thought he was fulfilling his fantasy, but really he was sleeping with the same woman over and over again, for it was Fantomina who dressed up as a different woman each time. Maybe if Tulsi were to conceive a little game of her own and turn herself into a hundred orgasmic women, one of them would conceive.

'How did I do today?' she asked.

'You did very well,' I told her. Now run home to your husband.

'Thank you,' she repeated, 'thank you, thank you!' and left like a dart that would land a micrometre away from the target yet again.

She walked to her little red car parked next to the chromatic teashop that sold double-strong tea and Kings. She was oblivious to the Tamil film music blaring on the radio and the eyes that were riveted on her as she walked past them and sat in her car. Next month, the little red car would be back, parked under the same coconut tree next to the same mottled teashop, and she would walk into my consultation room and ask me the same question.

Leela sat next to her mother, wearing a pastel green shirt dotted with yellow flowers, her stomach puffed up. She sat up straight, her head slightly tilted to one side, like a violinist poised before a conductor. I was waiting to hear the music.

She looked at me as if she were looking through me at the calendar behind me. And then she smiled ever so gently. I have never fallen down, her smile seemed to say. I have never spilt a glass of milk. I have never stained my dress. Because, I thought, you would have to run with all your heart, down a mountain slope with gravity on your side, to fall down.

Leela was spotless. Her jet-black hair was pulled back in an immaculate knot. Her face was like the full moon on a starless night and on her large forehead was a black bindi the size of a mustard seed. Her sindoor was reduced to a tenth of its size and glued to her forehead like a full stop.

Leela was a science student. She couldn't walk around in a cherry-sized bindi like her mother did. She had studied in a convent. She used to recite the Lord's Prayer at school and numerous lords' prayers at home and had always wondered why there were so many lords. And when India won the World Cup in 1983, she was one confused little girl – yet another Lords! But for all the moral science lessons at Sacred Heart School, the Nativity plays she had acted in (mostly as an obscure angel standing close to the wings), and her weekly visits to the school church (where she had been appalled to see the emaciated lord for the first time, stripped and nailed to a wooden cross), she was quite faithful to her dolled up domestic lords. She prayed to Saraswati for wisdom, Lakshmi for wealth, the broken-tusked Ganesha to toss away obstacles in her path, and when she got married she prayed to baby Krishna for a baby.

She was not ready, she wanted to focus on her career, but her mother-in-law had given her the little idol on her wedding night and asked her to feed it milk in the morning. Leela had obliged and, much to her dismay, she conceived within a week.

'Pottu vechiko!' her mother would scream from the kitchen as she left for school in starched green uniform. 'Pottu vechiko!' her mother would scream from the gate as she left for college in jeans and t-shirt. So she developed the art of pasting a microscopic pottu right in the middle of her forehead. The glue from her sticker bindi left an indelible white mark on her forehead and sometimes it itched. Why do women wear bindis, she often wondered. What does the sanctimonious dot signify?

One day during the summer holidays when she was twelve years old, she decided to look up the Sanskrit dictionary in her grandfather's house. It was in the inky room where her great-grandfather lay talking to himself and drinking buttermilk loaded with asafoetida. She tiptoed into the room and pulled out the fat Sanskrit-English dictionary from the rotating rosewood bookshelf. *Bind, Binda, Bindu…*

Her great-grandfather was blind. He lay in a corner mumbling something and somehow he knew she was in the room.

'What are you looking for, Leela kutti?' he asked.

'Bindi,' she said.

'For that you have to look in the ladies' chambers,' he said in a queer Victorian accent, the only vestige of his civil service during the Raj.

'I am looking for the meaning of the word.'

He sat up and smiled. For a moment she could have sworn he wasn't blind. She said she wanted to know why a bindi was worn. He looked into her eyes and cleared his throat several times. She felt so scared that she turned around to slip away.

'It implies the mystical third eye of a person,' he said finally.

'What's that?'

'We all have two eyes that look at the world. We also have a third one that looks inward. It is the eye of the mind.'

It sounded fascinating and scary at the same time. She wondered if he was looking at her with his third eye. She had heard that her great-grandfather was a great yogi. He could stand on his head. He could coil his leg around his neck and sit like that for hours on end. But she had also heard that he was senile now.

'But why is the bindi worn?' she asked.

'When the kundalini is awakened during meditation, it travels from the base of the spine to the seventh chakra on the head and the area between the eyebrows is an exit point for this potent energy.'

'So if you put a bindi there, it cannot escape?'

'Spoken like the great-granddaughter of a true bio-mechanic,' he said and coiled himself up and went to sleep.

Her mother-in-law had told her something very different. A married woman wears the pottu, she had snapped the day Leela forgot to wear the dot, to express her desire for her husband's longevity. Don't you know the goddess Parvati protects men whose wives apply vermilion? And who protects *them*, Leela wondered.

But she wore a bindi because her mother wore a bindi, because her grandmother wore a bindi, because her great-

...er had worn a bindi and because she had always
...di, because deep in the pit of her swollen stomach
sat a superstitious little stooge who said that if she didn't
wear one it would bring her misfortune.

If indeed it were for the longevity of her husband, I
thought, it beat starving an entire day as some married
women do in northern India. On the fourth night after the
full moon in the month of Karthik in the Hindu calendar,
they begin fasting just after the appearance of the moon and
wait until the next night's moonrise to break the fast. Often
there is a fast-breaking ceremony when the women dress up
and go to the terrace to look at the moon before looking at
their husband's face. What would the immortal husband do
after that? How would he pay up for the starvation? Would
he carry her down the steps and kiss her gently? Would he
make love to her slowly and steadily, and then ride her like
a supersonic train till she came and came again?

Or would *he* come and go to sleep?

I did an ultrasound and found out what I had already
guessed. It was a girl. She had had a boy first and now three
years later she was going to have a girl. I could imagine her
with two oily pigtails, one black dot on her forehead and
one on her cheek. What a happy little girl she would be, I
thought, but how terribly wrong I was.

I scheduled Leela's check-ups till her due date. I booked a
room for her delivery. It was on the first floor at the back of
the building with a view of the metro trains that fly across the
bridge. If you used your imagination you would see the sea
beyond the trains and if you looked really hard, you would
see paper boats floating in the sea, made out of newspapers
 and magazines, and in one paper boat in the sea, you would
read your horoscope for the week.

But Leela didn't see the sea. She didn't even see the trains. Maybe if she had looked with her little black bindi, she would have seen it all.

———

He was the cricket captain of the school team, Pooja said. He was six feet tall and everybody looked up to him. When she walked with him, it was like walking in the grass with bare feet. You could feel every step.

She would stay back after basketball practice until he finished cricket. She would walk slowly till he caught up with her. She giggled when he told her she was the prettiest girl in the school and when they talked about botany and bowling, TV and the Third World War, Slim Shady and Shakespeare, but the day he kissed her behind the chemistry lab and something imploded inside her, she didn't giggle.

Suddenly everything changed. She became the girlfriend of the cricket captain. It was not easy being the girlfriend of the cricket captain. Everybody knew him. Everybody loved him. She needed to be known and loved too. So she coloured her hair burgundy and took her skirt two inches up. She lived on love and fresh air and knocked off a few kilos. But that was the easy part. What took the life out of her were the games she had to play. She had to play basketball like Michael Jordan. She had to leave the ground and hang in the air and only then would he think of her.

They kissed again; behind the chemistry lab, behind the school library, behind the gulmohar tree in the cricket ground. One day he took her to the terrace of his five-storey building and when the toy houses disappeared from her view, he lay her down gently and made love to her on the hard concrete floor.

One month went by and suddenly her period was like a grandfather clock that had stopped chiming. She wanted to hear it chime, she wanted to hear it tick, but it stood still. Another month passed and she went with her best friend to the pharmacy and bought a pregnancy test. She took it home, hidden inside her chemistry notebook. She peed into a jar and took a dropper with tottering fingers, dipped it into the jar and took out three little drops of pee. She dropped it into the test. Three minutes later, she peeped at the test window and saw a purple line, one where it was supposed to be and a second one right next to it, almost psychedelic, as if her soul had manifested itself onto that line.

Since then she had been carrying it in the ghettos of her belly. Now she sat fidgeting in her chair and gave me forlorn glances from time to time. I found out that her last period was two-and-a-half months ago. Once her ultrasound showed that it was an intrauterine pregnancy, I could go ahead with the abortion. But I would have to break the law.

According to the Medical Termination of Pregnancy Act, there are two conditions under which a pregnancy can be terminated: when a pregnant woman has a serious medical condition and the continuation of pregnancy can endanger her life and when the continuation of pregnancy can lead to substantial risk to the newborn, causing serious physical or mental handicap. As neither was the case and she was below eighteen years of age, I would need the written consent of her guardian.

'Can't we do it out now?' she cried out. 'I just want it out of me!'

'You need to do some tests first.'

'I do a lot of them in school.'

'Then you need an ultrasound.'

'An ultrasound?' she giggled nervously. 'That sounds ultramodern.'

By now she was laughing like a bobbing head doll with tears streaming down her cheeks. She needed medication to calm her down. She needed someone by her side.

'You should ask him to come with you,' I told her.

'He's gone,' she said and her head began to bobble again, as if someone had tapped it playfully.

———

Megha was wearing an orange chiffon sari with purple flowers. She looked skinnier than the last time I saw her. She looked so absurdly thin that the purple flowers looked like they had sprung from her skin. On the parting of her hair was bright red sindoor, as if to signal to passers-by that the road on her scalp was blocked. Caution. Woman at work.

She was pregnant again.

'She have to have boy,' her mother-in-law said.

I noted her last period in her medical file and asked her mother-in-law to leave so I could do an internal exam. She waddled away and as soon as she left, Megha caught hold of my hand with her skeletal white fingers.

'Doctor,' she said, 'I have to have son.'

I opened my mouth in anger but stopped when I saw her face. Her large eyes looked absurd in that tiny little face and her lips barely moved when she spoke.

'I am having two daughters. If I give them one son, maybe they will treat me like I exist,' she said and disappeared into the teakwood chair.

She was like a peppered moth camouflaged against a predatory bird and like the moth before a flame she stood before a stove making over a hundred rotis every day, rolling the dough into circles, dusting them with flour, roasting them on both sides, holding them one by one over the flame with her bare hands. The children would eat them first with cream and sugar and then her husband would swallow them whole with his father and brother, after that the demon duck of doom would make her entrance as if from a frozen lake and fresh hot rotis would be served to her, and finally, Megha would eat them with her lifeless hands, soaking pieces in whatever she found, a little yellow dal here, a little red gravy there, and everybody would disappear into the sky like helium balloons on a beach: her mother-in-law, her father-in-law, her husband, her brother-in-law, her sister-in-law, her little nephews and even her daughters, her sweet little daughters, even they would disappear.

And then she would cry, for she would remember her mother making rotis, spinning them around like the Ferris wheel in a fair, rising a hundred feet above the ground and then coming down. She never wanted to come down the giant wheel in the fair, she wanted to stay in the air like a bird while her mother stood on the ground spinning the gigantic wheel with her pathetic little hands. If she ever came down, it would be to enter a carousel with flying horses. She hadn't imagined then that there would be demon ducks of doom who didn't know that all animals were equal.

In the straggling white mansion in the north of Chennai with a red swastika above the front door, above the Poonamallee High Road where the Dasaprakash Hotel once captivated Madrasis with its bread peas masala and 'venne-nila' ice-cream, men were more equal than women.

Aristotle said that a female is female by virtue of a certain lack of qualities and we should regard the female nature as afflicted with a natural defectiveness. He also thought the earth stood motionless at the centre of the universe. And he lived in 300 BC. We were living in the twenty-first century, in a city that had changed its name but not its face. Here the lowest temperature recorded is over fifteen degrees and the highest building built is under fifteen storeys. Here people wake up at the crack of dawn to draw a kolam on their doorstep and a pottu on their forehead. People stop at a streetside shrine to have a conversation with a bejewelled god but walk past each other without so much as a nod. While the city still clings to its Tamil heritage like plastic wrap to a dosa, it also has the latest gizmos, tech toys, cars and bars, and seven-and-a-half million hearts beating every day.

How did she fit into all this, I wondered, this incongruously shaped woman with eyes like jellyfish? What was her story? She reminded me of that pale woman on the cover of *Tess of the d'Urbervilles*. Was it because her family was poor and her face was her trumpcard that she was forced into an arranged marriage to a wealthy family; the beautiful daughter sold to a stranger in return for a lifetime of saris and pooris? Like Tess she didn't do great things, like Tess her life was torn to little shreds while she continued living in two dimensions.

'We'll do everything we can for you to have a healthy baby,' I said finally, 'and we'll hope it's a boy.'

—

Anjolie was reading me like the Sunday paper. Then she smiled. Her teeth looked like pearls in an oyster. I have fallen, her smile said. I have fallen over and over, but somehow I pick myself up.

Her red khadi skirt wrapped her body seductively. She had a tight bottom that came from twenty years of Hatha yoga and performance art. Had Freddy Mercury seen her through his mascara, he would have changed the words of his song. 'Tight-bottomed girls,' he would have sung instead, 'you make the rocking world go round.'

'I would like to find out if my reproductive organs are fine,' she said, matter of fact.

She was thirty-two and not a year of it showed on her crystalline face. I have seen several beautiful women before. I have seen their faces, their bellies, their breasts, their vaginas and what lies underneath. But what was it about her face that took my breath away? It wasn't her skin that looked like a peach blossom, it wasn't her fish-shaped eyes that were swimming before mine, it wasn't her nose that was moulded from a parrot's beak, it wasn't her pearl-like teeth. It was something else.

It was four in the afternoon and the sun shone through the translucent yellow curtains, bathing the consultation room with its tainted light. The calendar was pale orange, the Doppler was ruby-red as if numerous foetal hearts were beating away inside it, and my teakwood desk looked like an orange tree.

'Why do you think there's something wrong with your reproductive organs?' I asked.

'I've done a lot of things to my body while practising my art,' she said and searched my face for a reaction.

I looked into her eyes. They were like a kaleidoscope. As I looked in one end, light entered the other end and reflected off a thousand mirrors and when I turned my head, I saw colours and patterns I had never seen before.

'I've had two miscarriages,' she continued. 'And I've been trying to have a baby for a few years.'

So that was why she was here, to find out if she could

have a baby, to find out if she could breathe into the pain and break the waters and blow out a bundle of joy.

She pulled her hair back and bunched it into a knot the size of a melon. The last one was two years ago, she said. She was in New York giving a lecture at Columbia University on performance and video art and suddenly the screen went out of focus and she started cramping. She bled all the way to St Luke's Hospital, where the doctor confirmed her fears. She had lost her baby. They did a D&C, and just like that, in the time it takes to say those two letters, it was gone and all that was left in her hands were several little lifelines crisscrossing each other.

The story of her miscarriage was like the Mahabharata to me. I had heard it a thousand times within the walls of this room from a motley of storytellers: receptionists and reporters, lawyers, cashiers and dancers, mothers with babies who wanted another one, wives of school teachers who couldn't afford another one.

So why is Anjolie's story significant? Why does Megha strike a chord when dozens of women like her come to me with their own demon ducks of doom? What makes Tulsi special when hundreds of women grapple with infertility? And Zubeida? Aren't there enough and more women having babies again and again and again? Why did I choose these women over the hundreds of others who come to me? Why do I tell their stories? Because their lives were intertwined like fibres braided together in a rope. When Zubeida sighed, Megha sighed unknowingly at the other end of this checkered city; when Tulsi cried, Anjolie laughed and when Pooja embraced a brave new world, Leela slipped out of hers.

Although they opened their hearts to me, they were like the cast of an absurd play. What happened offstage, behind closed doors, I could only speculate. I couldn't go to their homes and observe them from there and even if I could, wouldn't they change their behaviour if I were there?

This is one of the inherent problems with subatomic systems too: the difficulty of human observation. One can assume that subatomic particles behave in a certain way but observing them in action can affect the natural behaviour of these particles.

I thought of Schrödinger's cat: the thought experiment proposed by Erwin Schrödinger in 1935. We put a cat into a steel box along with a device containing a vial of hydrocyanic acid. There is a very small amount of a radioactive substance inside the box. If even a single atom of the substance decays during the test period, a relay mechanism will trip a hammer, which will in turn break the vial and kill the cat. The observer cannot know whether or not an atom of the substance has decayed and, consequently, cannot know whether the vial has been broken, the hydrocyanic acid released and the cat killed. Since we cannot know, the cat is both dead and alive in a superposition of states, according to quantum law. It is only when we break open the box and observe the condition of the cat that the superposition is lost and the cat becomes either dead or alive.

These women were like Schrödinger's cat. I never saw them outside this consultation room. I never saw them inside their box. And so, to tell you the whole story, I would have to break open that box and look inside.

Three for a girl,
Four for a boy

3

Zubeida felt a butterfly in her stomach as she leaned over the railing to pull out the clothes that were hanging on two black lines parallel to the cement wall. She was fourteen weeks pregnant. She had had three sons and this time she knew it was going to be a girl. Only a girl can flutter like this, she thought and smiled to herself.

Her faded brown petticoat was flapping against the wall. The evening sunlight fell on the folds, turning them into golden brown feathers, and she unclipped the animated garment from the line and pulled it out. It was warm, like her heart, like her belly button tucked inside pleats of crumpled sari. She pulled out overstretched underwear and socks. She pulled out shirts and trousers. She pulled out her bottle-green kurta with paisley prints on the border. The paisleys looked like little embryos stacked on a windowsill. Her baby would be crouched like a paisley and pumping blood, about twenty-five quarts a day. She knew this because she had read an article in *The Hindu* called the 'Amazing Journey of Pregnancy', though she didn't think pregnancy was a journey to begin with.

As she folded the misfortunes of mankind neatly into a pile and left hope hanging on the line, she saw a minaret of the Wallajah mosque between a cloud and a patch of sky. She had read that the tallest minaret in the world was in Casablanca. As the muezzin called to prayer, she saw people rolling out their prayer mats in the direction of the Qibla.

Her husband had gone for his evening prayers with his two younger brothers. Ramadan was three days away. Her husband had told her that god exempted pregnant and lactating women and travellers from fasting. She wished she were a traveller, on her way to Casablanca perhaps, and not a pregnant woman. Then she smiled secretly, thinking, this time it would be different, this time it would be a girl and she would finally be the mother she never had. Besides, she thought, her smile widening, she didn't have to fast this Ramadan.

The boys were playing with a toy train on skimpy tracks. There was no one else at home. Ever since her mother-in-law died, she stopped performing the prayers but the men went to the mosque after washing themselves several times and rubbing their heads with water.

'The whole body with the nostrils, mouth and head must be washed by a complete bath in any of the following cases,' her husband had told her on their wedding night. 'One, after intimate intercourse.' They had intercourse thrice a day. His appetite for sex had shocked her at first but in time it became a sort of ritual, like the prayers. She would close her eyes and perform in bed as she had performed prayers all her life: eyes gently closed, thinking about parakeets, parachutes and Paris.

She had read a review of Paris hotels in *The Hindu* that morning. 'Paris Hotels: How to Reduce the Risk of Selecting the Wrong Hotel', the article said. Hôtel de Lille: an art deco-inspired hotel right behind the Louvre. Hôtel des Arts: right on top of the Montmartre Hill. Hôtel de Londres Eiffel: two minutes from the Eiffel Tower.

'Two, after wet dreams…' he had told her. She wondered who he was dreaming about when he had a wet dream. Was it a woman in a tight red dress? Or a woman in an oversized burqa?

Mustafa was kind. He was a fair, bespectacled man whose overgrown beard made him look much older than his thirty-six years. He owned a lehenga shop near the mosque and sold silk and georgette lehengas in dazzling colours. His life, however, lacked colour. It was one monotonous sentence punctuated by sex and prayers.

He adored his wife. He adored the way she sang in the shower, he adored the way her eyes lit up when he took her to the cinema, and he adored her smile most of all. He would never let another man see it.

'Zoo,' he would call her while making love, his breath smelling of mutton biryani. 'Zoo,' he would call her while sitting at the dining table when he wanted another piece of chicken. He was full of zoo, she thought, but he had never been to one. She had been to the zoo when she was a little girl with her cousins, her aunts trailing behind them like baby elephants in burqas. It was the early eighties and they thought the zoo was still in Park Town. They had taken the bus from Royapettah to Parry's Corner and when her aunt asked the conductor for eight tickets to Parry's, Zubeida thought they were going to Paris. Paris, she thought, looking at the bright pink tickets, is just a few bus stops away.

But the zoo was not in Parry's. It had expanded so much that they had to move it out of the city, and the wolves, jackals, deer, hyenas, elephants, tigers, lions, panthers, giraffes, camels, bears and star tortoises had moved to Vandalur, thirty-five kilometres away. Zubeida wondered how the animals had gone there. Did they travel by bus with bright pink tickets from Paris?

Her husband couldn't care less. He had never seen a zebra. He had never seen a giraffe. Not even in picture books where they were orange like the sun. Mustafa Zainuddin had never read a book in his life. The only thing he read were the classifieds in *The Hindu*. 'Lost and Found' was his favoured category, closely followed by 'Change of Name'. But for Zubeida, the only thing she *could* read was *The Hindu*. She loved to read. When she walked back home from school with her cousins, she would beg them to wait for her while she dashed into the Eshwari Lending Library on Lloyds Road to return an old book and borrow a new one. The last book she had borrowed was *To Kill a Mockingbird*.

That bloody Monday morning when her father told her she wouldn't be going to school any more, she was already in her uniform with her school bag across her shoulders, and in that bag, among the science books and history, was an old paperback of *To Kill a Mockingbird*. She never returned the book. She read it several times over the years until she could recite it like the Holy Quran. Just as Muslims regarded the Quran as god's final revelation to mankind, she regarded her book as the world's final revelation to her.

'When he was nearly thirteen, my brother Jem got his arm badly broken at the elbow,' she would recite. 'When it healed, and Jem's fears of never being able to play football were assuaged, he was seldom self-conscious about his injury. His left arm was somewhat shorter than his right; when he stood or walked, the back of his hand was at right angles to his body, his thumb parallel to his thigh. He couldn't have cared less, so long as he could pass and punt.'

That awful Monday morning, she stepped out of her canvas shoes for the last time and took out the book from her schoolbag. She read it from cover to cover and when it was over, she spotted a newspaper lying on the sofa. When her father went to bed, she sneaked into the sofa room and picked up the abandoned *Hindu* and read every word. From that day, she held onto the newspaper like a puppeteer to his strings and lived within those twenty-four pages that were larger than life. She read it till she was married off to the merchant with a beard and a soft corner for her and on their wedding night when they were bathing after sex – she bleeding between her thighs, he washing his sacred penis with a powder-pink bar of Lux soap – he told her to ask him for anything she wanted. And so Zubeida asked him for *The Hindu* on their first night of holy matrimony.

It was only natural that Mustafa was shocked. 'Which Hindu do you want?' he cried out, stopping his sacred ablution, for he thought she was talking about *a* Hindu. But when she told him that she was talking about a newspaper, he laughed out loud and subscribed to it the very next day. She never asked him for anything after that. She cooked and cleaned the house, she made the beds, she nursed their sons. She didn't go out, except to go to the market to buy tomatoes and onions. She couldn't have cared less, she told herself, so long as she could think and feel, so long as she could read.

Zubeida peeled an enormous purple onion, chopped it into little pieces and dumped it into a bowl of curd with a pinch of salt. She shredded the coriander leaves and sprinkled it over the dal gosht. She tasted the beef korma. It was delightful.

She went to the living room and opened the multicoloured *Young World*. Below an article that explained how to fold paper into rockets and make them fly was a poem written by a thirteen-year-old girl. That's how old *she* was, she thought, on the day that changed her life.

> *The fisherman's daughter looked at the sea*
> *She looked and looked at the sea-blue sea*
> *And wondered about the mountains*
> *The mountain goats on mountain tops*
> *And being so high you can almost touch the sky.*
> *Miles away in the mountains*
> *High up there in the mountains*
> *The tea-picker's daughter looked at the sky*
> *She looked and looked at the sky-blue sky*
> *And wondered about the sea*
> *The seashells and seagulls*
> *And swimming so free in the sea.*

How wrong the little girl in *Young World* was, she thought.

Zubeida lived in Triplicane, an anglicized name for Tiruvallikeni, which meant 'sacred lily pond'. She felt like she really was living in a sacred lily pond, trapped on one side by the Wallajah mosque and on the other by the Parthasarathy temple where young women wore nine yards and a bright red line split their heads into two. She imagined herself in nine yards of bright Kancheepuram, her long hair in a braid with jasmines tucked into it, a blood red line running down her scalp. She would look pretty, she thought, and fat. She was living in a sacred lily pond, just half a kilometre from the Bay of Bengal, trapped in a pool of sanctity, and she could walk to the ocean in ten minutes flat. But she had never walked to the ocean. She had never swum in the sea. How wrong she was, the little girl in *Young World*. She too would get her period and grow up.

Her boys were fighting over a race car with missing wheels. Her younger son began to suck his thumb. It was time to put them to bed, so she dragged them to the king-sized bed that they all slept in together. She read to them the story of *Goldilocks and the Three Bears*.

'Once upon a time, there was a little girl called Goldilocks. She went for a walk in the woods and came upon a house. She knocked on the door and when no one answered, she went inside.'

They played with their dog-eared pillows. She read. They played. She read.

'Goldilocks woke up and saw the three bears standing in front of her. She jumped up and ran out of the room. She ran down the stairs, opened the door, and ran into the woods. And she never returned to the house of the three bears.'

The doorbell rang.

The three of them were home.

———

MR FERRARI DRIVES A FIAT.

So said the ad in the big black book. Tulsi loved to read good copy. She liked headlines that made her smile. Like her husband, she thought, in his Levi's on her first day at the agency.

It was Dhruv's last day. He was leaning against the glass window in Creative and making a fish face at someone in the parking lot. He looked like an Olympian god in a pair of jeans. She looked at his ponytail and bottom and ponytail and bottom when suddenly he turned and caught her staring. He smiled like a schoolboy who had just found a balloon.

'Come to my party, sweetie,' he said.

Should I say yes, she wondered, looking into his scintillating brown eyes. But she barely knew him. And if I say no, she thought, looking away, I'll never get to know him.

'I have to get perm,' she said finally.

'But your hair looks lovely,' he said. 'I wouldn't get a perm if I were you.'

'I mean I have to get permission to party,' she said, tucking her straight brown hair behind her ears.

She was nineteen and just out of college. She had to get her parents' permission for parties. Her dad would consent, but her menopausal mum would throw a fit. If she went to the party that night, she wouldn't get permission to go out for two Saturday nights in a row. Now *that* was something to consider. She would have to spend two Saturday nights at home beside the reading lamp instead. But why did she even want to go to this party? She didn't know anybody. She had spoken to all of two copywriters who looked like they spoke a lot less than they wrote (and they didn't write very much) and an art director who doodled all over himself. So why did she want to go? Something told her that if she didn't go to the party that night, she would never see Dhruv again.

'Get yourself a perm if you must,' he said, grinning from ear to ear, 'but come tonight.

'It's Number 7, 2nd Cross Street, Besant Nagar,' he mouthed as he turned to run down to the person he was making fish faces at. 'We're on the third floor next to the rickety lift!' he shouted from the staircase.

Before she could reply, he was gone – like a Cheshire cat from a treetop – and astonishingly, he had left his grin behind. Tulsi sat in front of the empty window, thinking that she had often seen a man without a grin but never a grin without a man.

She looked into the giant black book and read the iconic British Airways ad: *Children walk to school and run back home.* Did she ever run back home, she wondered. She just moved from one kendriya vidyalaya to the next, wearing the same navy-blue skirt and white blouse. Her father worked for Northern Railways and her family moved from one small north Indian town to the other but every summer they came back to Madras, to her grandmother's house with its red floors and green windows from which you could see coconut trees. When she was ten years old, her father was transferred to New Delhi and she joined sixth standard in DPS R.K. Puram. Even though most of her classmates could draw the map of India with their eyes closed, they still thought that if you came from the south, you were a Madrasi. She would patiently explain to them that Andhra Pradesh, Karnataka and Kerala were independent states with capitals of their own. Madras is the capital of Tamil Nadu *only*, she would stress, pointing at the city in the map of India that hung next to the blackboard. But they never got it. She was just a Madrasi like half a dozen others in her class. And some of them hadn't even *been* to Madras!

When she finished school, her father's posting with Northern Railways ended and the family moved to Madras. Her brother went to the States to study. They lived in a large colonial house on Sterling Road and she would look at the coconut trees through the massive white windows and think about the coconuts she and her brother ate when they

were children, scooping out the translucent white flesh with
their hands.

She studied Fine Arts at Stella Maris. She made
watercolours of the sky. She made oils of the earth. She
read every word in her *History of Art* book and one night
she dreamt that she was sleeping next to Van Gogh in a bed
of sunflowers. Another night, when she fell asleep on the
couch in the living room, she dreamt that she was Picasso's
coal-eyed mistress in a painting and suddenly the hand that
was folded under her slight double chin covered her left eye
as if she were wiping away tears. When she woke up, her
eyes really were wet.

She would wake up from dreams about painters and
paint; she would paint sunflowers, she would paint roses,
but all she could show at the end of the day were perfect
little flowers on a canvas. So she joined advertising.

Tulsi twiddled her thumbs. She listened to conversations.
The phone rang. Somebody picked it up and said that Dhruv
was out for lunch. He'll come back, she thought excitedly,
and as the light from the window fell on the book, the copy
stood out against a phosphorescent page.

*A FEW ENCOURAGING WORDS FOR THE TOTALLY
INCOMPETENT. It's perfectly all right to be incompetent for
hours on end.* That's great, thought Tulsi, I'm in the right
place. *I am and so is everyone I know. Of course, being of this
persuasion, I shall never be able to afford a bottle of Beck's Beer.
Which is why the people who sell Beck's Beer got me to write
this ad.*

'Dhruv's not coming back,' somebody said behind her.

Tulsi stopped reading.

'I mean from Bombay, da. He's going to become a rock
star.'

'He'll have more girlfriends now,' said one of the art directors from his chair.

'Oh, yes he will, that old rascal,' said the creative director coming out of his cabin, 'that old rascal who writes the best copy around here.'

'Now nobody will be adding rum to my kaapi,' said the disappointed coffee boy, pouring coffee back and forth between two coffee cups and creating stunning patterns of coffee bubbles.

Precisely at that moment, Dhruv came back to the office from what seemed like an extended beer lunch without the lunch. He took out a bottle of Old Monk from his desk, poured some rum into his kaapi as if to please the coffee boy and smiled at Tulsi.

She would fly to the party that night, she thought. She would find Number 7, 2nd Cross Street, and leap to the third floor. She would land on his shoulders and eat his heart out.

———

MR FERRARI DRIVES A FIAT. Or so said the ad in the dusty old black book. That was eleven-and-a-half years ago, Tulsi thought. Then Dhruv drove a Fiat.

She looked through the same window in Creative at the same parking lot. His Accent entered the compound. An Esteem backed out. He had great parking karma, she thought, an uncanny ability to find the perfect parking spot. Even when they played Monopoly he got Free Parking. He would collect fifty dollars from every player and all she had ever won was second prize in a beauty contest. But in real life, Dhruv had given money to every player and come back from Bombay without a band. Tulsi had waited for him at

Central Station with sandwiches and a bottle of wine and they went to his old apartment in Besant Nagar and made love all afternoon. That night, he asked her to marry him and she said yes. She promptly knocked off her maiden name. Now she was Tulsi Schumacher. When they got married, Michael Schumacher had just made his Formula One debut and most people hadn't heard of him. She thought it sounded rather cool, she didn't know then that it was an occupational German surname for shoemaker (Dhruv's paternal grandfather was German and a *dress*maker) and she certainly didn't know that Michael Schumacher would become the most successful driver in Formula One history and that racing would become such a popular sport in India, that this unusual surname that was her husband's would be on everyone's lips and that people would tease her for the rest of her life and call her Frau Schumacher. If she had known she wouldn't have changed her name.

She turned a few pages. She could hear Carol, the Anglo-Indian receptionist, laughing. Dhruv had entered the building. The production manager guffawed and dropped something on the floor. He was in Production now. Dhruv was like a seismic wave travelling through the earth after a quake of ten on the Richter scale. He went from one department to another, making everybody laugh. It wasn't what he said that was funny, it was how he said it. His eyes would twinkle and you would laugh your heart out.

'Hey, you,' he said to Tulsi, who was still hiding behind the black book.

'Did you buy the groceries?'

'All twelve things on the list.'

'You found olives?'

'Sliced, black. Del Monte. Since 1892.'

'Great, I'll make pasta tonight.'

'Great, I'll get a bottle of wine.'

'Get two,' she said, her eyes sparkling. 'I'm coming home early.'

'I have to run,' he said. 'I have a meeting with a client for a commercial for flavoured condoms.'

She wondered what flavours they came in. They hadn't used a condom in years. They had been trying to have a baby for so long that the magic had gone out of the sex and something in her had died, something below her Armani belt and inside her Lovable panties. But what she didn't realize was that it had died for him too.

When he finally came out of the conference room a few hours later, Dhruv looked at Tulsi mischievously.

'I have tons of free samples,' he whispered. 'Let's try one tonight.'

'Why would you say that?' she asked him. 'Why on earth would you want to make love wearing a condom when we are trying so hard to have a baby?'

'Because it smells like oranges from China,' he said.

That was why she loved him: for his ability to live in the moment, wanting nothing more from life than that one moment he was living in. He was a rock star without a band; he had said that he would never go back to advertising yet here he was. He was living in the moment and basking in it as if it were sunshine.

Dhruv looked at Tara, the pretty film executive. She had orange streaks in her hair and a cut gone horribly wrong. She was sitting at her desk and looking woefully into the ceiling.

'Now I know there's *something* that can look bad on you!' he said to her with a naughty smile.

Tara's face lit up. She laughed and punched him in the chest.

'Now we *have* to look at your pretty face. We can't look at that hair.'

'As long as you're looking.'

Dhruv said bye to everyone and squeezed Tulsi's shoulders on the way out. Tara picked up her abandoned phone and went on with her day with the realization that a bad haircut was not the end of the world. She pushed her carrot bangs from her face and tucked them behind her ears to reveal a deeply dimpled smile.

Dhruv had left his grin behind again.

———

Leela was walking back home under a bright blue sky with her little boy tugging at her hand and another one tugging at her belly from the inside. The narrow pavement was dotted with trees and she alternated between the street and the pavement as her son jumped from one to the other gleefully. She heard the sound of anklets behind her. It was a freshly bathed bull walking with its master in tow, its horns painted pink, its back decorated with a tangerine yellow sari and garlanded with roses. The shops were all closed, the shutters pulled down and locked tight for Pongal. Leela walked past the shops, past the houses, scurrying down the street in a rhythm of her own. A little girl ran past her in her panties. Suddenly she was a little girl again. She was running naked on the beach and her mother was calling out her name. Leeeeeeeeeeeee-la! Wear your frock! And she was running, away from the sea, to where her mother sat holding a pink frock with pink sleeves. She ran to her mother and stepped into the frock.

'Do I have school today, amma?' her son asked, yanking
at her hand and bringing her back to the moment.

'No, kanna. You have four days' holidays for Pongal.'

'So that we can all eat pongal?'

Leela laughed and squeezed his hand. She explained to
him that Pongal was a dish *and* a festival.

'I don't have to go to school on festivals?'

'No, kanna, you don't.'

'And you don't have to go to office?'

'No.'

'Then you'll be with me the whole day!'

She lifted him up in the air and planted a big kiss on
his cheek. He giggled and she put him down and continued
walking, holding his precious little hand. In her other hand,
she clutched her purse that was now filled with turmeric roots
and she thought about what had happened that morning in
her mother-in-law's house. It all began so well. She walked
to her mother-in-law's house – the auspicious foot forward –
wearing an enormous red bindi on her forehead. She placed
the rice balls on turmeric leaves impeccably – red, yellow,
brown and white ones – in four straight lines, reciting: *Kaka
pidi vechen, kanu pidi vechen, kakakum kurivikum kalyanam. Kaka
pidi vechen, kanu pidi vechen, kakakum kurivikum kalyanam.*

Kakakum kurivikum kalyanam.

The crow and the sparrow are getting married.

Do their horoscopes match one hundred per cent, she
wondered.

When she was a year into her first job as a programmer
with a Fortune 500 company, her mother found her a suitable
boy. The planets were in the right place, the astrologer said.
His horoscope matches yours one hundred per cent, her
mother said. His name is Srinivasan, her father said; just

like yours, daddy, Leela thought and married him. Leela Srinivasan became Leela Srinivasan. She honeymooned in Lonavala and came back with packets of chikki and a bright orange sweater. But she shouldn't be thinking about that orange sweater, she thought, she should be thinking about how she had misplaced the turmeric *twice*.

The day before, her mother-in-law had given her a turmeric root to bring to the ceremony in the morning. After the women placed the rice balls on turmeric leaves one after the other – Leela in an unparalleled straight line – she asked for the turmeric root to rub into her cheeks and onto the sacred yellow thread dangling from her neck. But Leela had lost that turmeric root and brought another one. All it took was a cursory glance for her mother-in law to realize it was the wrong turmeric root. She was supposed to have brought the right one, the one her mother-in law had sanctified by tying around the Pongal pot. As though by smearing the yellowness of that turmeric root on her thaali and none other, she would enhance her husband's life by a hundred years. But she had brought the wrong one and her mother-in law glared at her and gave her another turmeric root. Leela prostrated numerous times before elders from her husband's family and each one gave her a fistful of rupees and more turmeric roots which she shoved into her purse. Then, unexpectedly, her ninety-nine-year-old grandmother-in-law, who usually lay supine in a corner all day, got up and stood in front of her and asked for the prostration *and* the turmeric root and she rummaged in her purse and pulled out long ones and short ones, fat ones and thin ones, straight ones and twisted ones, somehow missing the right turmeric root.

And now she was walking back home, with her little boy tugging at her hand, her baby tugging at her belly from the inside and something tugging at her heart that she couldn't put her finger on.

Today was the third day of Pongal when a married woman goes to her mother's house to perform the ceremony for the wellbeing of her brothers and to bond with her family. Why did her mother-in-law call her to *her* house? And what was it with all these turmeric roots, with all these rituals? Just when you got the hang of them, the whole point eluded you. And why were there so many of them? Why did she have to wake up at the crack of dawn on Deepavali and visit the whole jing-bang? Why couldn't she just revel in the holiday? And on Karthigai, why did she have to make countless murukkus? She was watching her calories, her husband had high cholesterol and her son hated murukkus. Who was she making them for? Oh, yes, she was making them for god, but god had never once taken a bite.

———

Pooja was sitting like a bat in the dark. Her feet seemed to be locked around an imaginary perch and she was hanging upside down in the air. If she fell, she would drop into the air. The lights came on and she sank a few inches lower into her seat. All around, people were beginning to get up from their seats to give a standing ovation. The movie had finally ended. It was the biggest hit of the year: *Dil Chahta Hai.* Her friends had seen it several times over but she couldn't focus on the film. She had sat through it alternating between the darkness and dissevered glimpses of Aamir Khan. She heard his voice a few times but by and large her ears were locked tight shut and her feet were locked tighter still around the imaginary perch that she was hanging from.

It was Anu who had insisted on taking her out in this predicament. You can't sit around and mope all day, she had said and dragged her to the movies. Pooja had pleaded with her to just let her be, let her lie in bed with the curtains drawn, but Anu wouldn't hear of it. This has gone on for weeks, she said, and the film will help you snap out of it. But the film hadn't helped her snap out of it, if you could snap out of these things to begin with.

She stood up and followed Anu into the crowd. They all looked like cartoon characters in slow motion, plodding down the aisle, talking animatedly as if they themselves had found love, and suddenly she felt jealous, jealous of everyone around her for their ability to find joy in cinema. For she couldn't find joy anywhere. She felt a great heaviness inside her as if Sunil himself was trapped in her heart and she was carrying him around. And of course, below her heart was another little thing that she was carrying around and although it weighed close to nothing, it was massive.

At first she had been angry when Sunil abandoned her, for not taking her calls, for disappearing on her while she carried part of him inside her, and then she felt an overwhelming sense of guilt because she had been lying to her mother and suddenly she wanted to lock herself in her room and cry. And now after the film, after watching people find love in a span of three hours, she wanted to find it too. She would call him one last time and he would come running to her like Aamir Khan. Maybe it had been too much for him, but now that some time had elapsed, perhaps he would come. Yes, that was what she was going to do. She would call him. Now that she had made up her mind, she felt wonderful, even excited, at the thought of dialling his number.

Outside the cinema, it was dazzling. It took time for her

eyes to get used to the brightness after sitting in the dark for so long. When they started walking towards the parking, Pooja put on her sunglasses and tapped Anu on the shoulder.

'I want to come to your place and try to call him one last time,' she whispered.

'You're most welcome to come home, babe,' Anu said, 'but calling him is not a good idea.'

'I know he loves me. It's just that he got scared after what happened.'

'You know what, you're probably right,' Anu said as they climbed onto her bright red Kinetic Honda. 'Maybe you should try one last time.'

'One last time.'

As they rode past the gates and got onto the road, they started to sing like old times, the light-hearted days before all this began and music still mattered and so did words. Pooja threw her head back and when they were on top of Gemini Flyover, she could see nothing but sky, a great expanse of solid sky. The blue calmed her nerves and the late afternoon sun acquired a pale orange glow through her tinted sunglasses. As they got closer to Anu's house in Nandanam, Pooja became anxious again as the decision of making one last call weighed on her with its possibilities. What if he was out? Would his mother give him the message? What if his mother didn't give him the message? Then what? Was she allowed another phone call?

They kicked off their shoes in the verandah and slipped into the house. It was a big old edifice with red oxide floors and solid wooden windows and the paint on the walls was almost colourless. Anu's mother came running behind them just as they were dashing off to Anu's room and asked them to eat tiffin.

'The idlis are piping hot,' she said. 'You girls need to eat. And just look at you, Pooja, you are losing too much weight!'

They followed her to the large rosewood dining table where Anu's grandparents sat licking sambar off their creased fingertips. The maid placed two steel plates for the girls and Pooja studied her reflection in the shiny plate. Had she really lost weight? The stainless steel extended her cheeks and tapered her forehead and what she saw was a gigantic mass of flesh staring back at her.

'No, thank you, aunty. Not for me,' Pooja said politely.

'No, no, you have to eat. These idlis will melt in your mouth!'

'But aunty, I ate a large sandwich at Sathyam while we were watching the film.'

Anu tried to say something but Pooja glared at her. Pooja had sat picking at popcorn and counting the calories in each kernel while Anu polished off a large chicken sandwich which she didn't get to eat at home. Anu's mother asked them about the film and Pooja tried to tell her the story, with vague pauses in between when she tried to recollect what she saw – or didn't see – while Anu gulped down four fluffy idlis.

And then they were off, up the staircase and into Anu's room in a second, locking the door behind them. Anu brought the cordless phone to Pooja with a wicked smile and Pooja held it in her hand, savouring this moment filled with hope, postponing the sorrow that might be lurking in the corner. Finally, she took a deep breath and began to dial the number, and the old familiar feeling came back. It was as if nothing had happened and her heart pounded with every ring as it always did when she called Sunil. And then he was there, at the other end of the line. She could picture his face as he picked up the phone and said hello.

'It's me.'

'Hi, Pooj.'

Oh, how her heart expanded as her name contracted when it came out of his mouth!

'Hi, Sunil. How are you?'

'I'm fine. What about you?'

'I'm as good as can be in these situations.'

'So what did the doctor say?'

'She told me to take some tests and come back. She told me to bring you along the day we do it.'

Sunil coughed and said he couldn't talk as his dad was right by the phone and they were in the middle of a family gathering.

'Why didn't you return my calls, Sunil?' Pooja asked. As soon as she said it she wished she hadn't.

'You know I'm studying for my entrance exams.'

'When did you take up studying, baby?' Pooja said and felt herself sink a few more inches.

'You wouldn't understand. You're not taking any entrance tests. You'll be through after boards. Some of us have to work hard.'

And some of us have to live hard, Pooja thought.

'So will you come with me the day we do it?'

'I'll tell you what, I'll come over tomorrow and see you and we'll figure it out. I gotta run now.'

'Bye, baby.'

'Bye.'

And that was it. With a click that resonated in her head, he was gone and she couldn't picture his face any more, but never mind, she said to herself; never mind, I'm going to see him tomorrow.

'What did he say?' Anu asked.

'He said he'll come over tomorrow and see me.'

'That's awesome! It was worth the wait, I guess. When is he coming?'

'I don't know. He didn't say.'

They lay on the bed, searching the ceiling for answers, and Pooja had a foreboding that this was the lull before the storm, this moment when nothing was said, nothing was done, just the two of them looking at the vacant ceiling.

Suddenly Anu jumped up and told her she had decided to study psychology.

'Have you decided what you want to do?'

Pooja wanted to make films. Not the ones where everyone finds love in the end. She wanted to make documentary films and she had already started thinking about her first one. It would be about pregnant teenage sex workers in Kamathipura.

'I want to go to the US to study film,' she replied.

'Wow! That sounds cool. Have you zeroed in on which schools to apply for?'

'Sort of,' she shrugged, trying to sound eager, but her mind was elsewhere.

It was in a little lane in Kilpauk behind the trees on top of the terrace of a five-storey building where a young girl was making love to a young boy for the first time. She didn't want to make love but she thought that if she did, he would love her. Oh, she loved to kiss him, how she loved to kiss him and cuddle him and even bite his neck like chocolate but when he unzipped her jeans and went inside, she looked up at the stars and wanted to cry.

Now she wanted to go home. She wanted to lie in bed with a pillow over her head. She waved goodbye to Anu and started walking down the street. The fluorescent street lamps looked like baby moons and she felt excited once again at the thought of seeing Sunil in the morning. A grumpy old auto-rickshaw driver pulled up.

'Greams Road,' she said and continued walking.

'Pipty rupees. Okay, vaa?'

She nodded and climbed inside. He darted off at great speed, skipping signals while she counted the streetlamps that hurtled past her. It started to rain and the driver unfolded two large plastic sheets over the sides of the auto-rickshaw and she sat in the dark and glided through the city.

———

Megha picked up the gooseberries from the verandah and put them in a bamboo basket. They had been drying on a newspaper in the sun for days. Now they were colourless and shrivelled up like her, ready to be marinated into pickle.

The smell of eggs frying in the neighbour's kitchen entered her nostrils and she wanted to vomit. She ran to the servant's latrine because that was the closest, positioned her face over the Indian-style pot and threw up her breakfast in one smooth elliptical movement from the gut.

She wanted to see her mother; her pasty, devoted mother with doe eyes and hollow cheeks around tiny lips that peeped out to kiss her in her dreams. Her face would break into a big smile when she saw Megha standing on the doorstep and Megha would spend all day following her mother around the house and narrating stories about the girls (never a word about her mother-in-law). But she would go back with the sun because otherwise people would think she had been discarded by her husband's family and they would talk in hushed tones and ask her when she was going back. She wondered what would happen if she told them she wasn't going back, she was *never* going back, she would stay in her mother's house.

Then her younger sister wouldn't get married.

What about the silk lehengas and sandalwood then? What about the feasts where she would sit at the head of the table, the ceremonies where she would be the centre of attention; the music, the dancing? It only lasted a day. Then the dholaks would stop playing, the shehnai would come to a halt, the priests would pack up and the wedding would be over. Everybody would go home, the musicians, the priests, the guests, the father of the bride, the mother, the sisters. The groom would go home too, and the bride would leave hers.

Megha picked up a cabbage with a firm head and peeled away the wilted outer leaves. She rinsed it under cold running water and cut the cabbage head in half. Her mother-in-law entered the kitchen and looked at her as if it were *her* head she was cutting.

'Buddhu!' she exclaimed. 'Don't you know cabbage is forbidden in chaturmash? Chaturmash started yesterday. I don't know how we took you into our family for that pathetic little sum and a TV set!'

Megha gathered all her courage and opened her mouth to say something to her mother-in-law, opening her mouth for the first time in five years, and at that precise moment her husband came home for lunch with his father and her mother-in-law waddled away to greet them. She threw the cabbage into the rubbish and peeped into the living room. Her husband was sitting on the sofa beside his father. Their oversized heads looked like eggs on their squat little bodies and Megha wondered which came first, the chicken or the egg.

But they didn't eat chicken. They didn't eat eggs. They didn't eat most root vegetables because they didn't kill whole plants unnecessarily. They were Jains.

She took the butcher knife that was dangling on a hook on the wall and chopped the tomatoes into fine pieces. She heated some oil in a pan and dropped mustard seeds with cloves, cinnamon and cumin. She added curry leaves and green chillies. She soaked tamarind in warm water and crushed it between her fingers, draining the juice from the tamarind flesh. She poured it into the sizzling pan. She added turmeric and red chilli powder. Chopped tomatoes. A pinch of salt. Finally she added the lentils that were soaking in water and let it boil over a slow flame.

She carried the dishes to the table one by one. Her father-in-law sat regally at the head of the table like Humpty Dumpty on the parapet wall. Today she was asked to sit at the table with them because she was carrying their precious little boy. Today it was her sister-in-law making hot chapattis in the kitchen. Everything was different today, for she had thrown up her breakfast and the family astrologer had told them that she was going to have a boy.

Chapattis were served one after another, first to her father in-law, then to her husband and to her brother-in-law, then to her mother-in-law who sat shaking her taffeta feathers, and finally to her. Then another cycle would begin and the chapattis would go around clockwise again, yielding to that inviolable order of centuries: first the men, in descending order of age, and then the women. But it was the other way round in Europe.

She was nine years old and hiding in her mother's
kitchen with two oily braids tied with nylon ribbons. Her
father had brought a European man home for tea. He took
photographs of their dingy little house and her mother made
tea for everyone. She served him first but he took the cup of
milky tea and offered it back to her.

'No, no, ladies first,' said the golden-haired man with a
smile.

'In India, we put the donkey last,' her grandfather said.

Everybody laughed: her grandfather, her uncles and her
father. Her mother laughed too. She didn't speak English.

That night Megha dreamt that her ears had grown long.
She tries to push them back but they keep growing. She
takes a lion's mask from under the bed and wears it over her
unwieldy head, covering her donkey face and donkey ears
until all she can see is the fearless face of a lion. Someone
calls her and she turns around with her spectacular mane
and opens her mouth to say something but what comes out
is an ear-splitting hee-haw.

The clock struck one. She was back in the present. She
was sitting at the table with her husband's family eating
chapattis. She served herself some dal in a katori with
unsteady hands and drank it in a single gulp. She burnt her
tongue. She fidgeted with the peas on her plate and dug her
tawny nails into a cold chapatti.

'Aap ande jaise lagte hain.' You look like an egg, she said
to Humpty Dumpty and everybody stared at her. Her voice
was barely audible and her mumbled words didn't come out
quite right. 'Aaj khana bahut achha hain.' The food is very
good today, she managed to say, finally uttering words that
were audible to human ears at a lunch table.

She finished the rest of her meal in seconds and excused

herself; excusing herself in a single moment for being a woman, excusing herself for her mother, her sisters and her daughters, excusing herself for not breeding sons.

'I thought she said something about an egg,' her father-in-law said.

He was fat on top and skinny on the bottom. You didn't know where his neck ended and the rest of him began and the cleft on his chin looked like a belly button on a paunch. Her husband was slowly putting on weight on his face and one day when her daughters were old enough to be married, he would be the splitting image of his father.

She went upstairs to the bedroom she shared with her husband and children. There was a large portrait of his great-grandfather hanging on the wall. The bottom of his head was larger than the top and she couldn't make out where his chin ended and the rest of him began. She stared at the portrait and for a moment it looked like it would fall off the wall.

'Now I know which came first,' she said to herself and lay down.

———

Anjolie kneeled on the floor. She leaned forward, placing her elbows, forearms and palms flat on the mat in front of her. She stretched her neck and tilted her head back. She raised her bottom and swung her legs in one swift movement over her head. She stayed like that in vrischika asana, her feet dangling in the air over her head, balancing herself on her forearms. She looked like a scorpion; she felt like a scorpion with its tail arched above its head, ready to sting its next victim.

She counted. One thousand, two thousand, three

thousand. She counted sheep and then some more sheep. She counted the men she had kissed. She counted him twice and then started all over again.

She had kissed him only once.

He had leaned forward to kiss her on the mouth but she moved her head back and looked into his eyes; she blinked; she looked; she blinked; and when he was about to move away, she kissed him at the edge of his lower lip. It was like kissing a brick wall at the edge of the universe and suddenly realizing that there is no brick wall, there is no edge to the universe; it is infinite, it goes on and on expanding until it collapses under its own gravity.

Anjolie came out of her pose gracefully. She had performed the vrischika asana at the Guggenheim Museum with a live scorpion crawling on her body. That had been her last performance. She had burnt out. She had thrown a blanket over the embers but she still remembered the first spark.

It was the late eighties. She was studying French at the Alliance Française on College Road. 'You'll connect with your dead father at least in language if not in spirit,' her mother had said while enrolling her. Every day after class she would go to the library and pore over endless volumes of art books. Between those four walls on the first floor, whether she connected with her dead father or not, she certainly connected with Cezanne, Monet, Matisse, Renoir, Lautrec and Van Gogh.

They changed the way she looked at her motionless walls and windows. They changed the way she looked at the sun on a sunny day, at a grape in a bowl of grapes; they changed the way she looked at life, her insignificant little life studying corporate secretaryship in the annexe of Ethiraj College and recipes at home while her mother sat by the window painting her toenails red.

Her mother met her father when he came to India with a broken guitar to learn transcendental meditation. He fell in love with her pretty brown face and took her with him to the Himalayas. She ran away from home with a bag of clothes and while they were crossing the Ganges on a little wooden boat, she vomited into the river and discovered she was pregnant. They got married in a temple at the edge of a frozen lake and nine months later she delivered a beautiful baby girl. *'Mon ange,'* he would call her, *'mon ange très très jolie,'* so they named her Anjolie. They travelled across the Himalayas with Anjolie. A year went by and he spent his guitar and money. Anjolie screamed in their arms, screamed for food and for the sound of music in her ears, so they took up odd-jobs in the foothills of the Himalayas (he guided French-speaking tourists and she the English-speaking ones). When they woke up one morning, tired and airless under a thatched roof, the passion had gone out of their home like the flame from their kerosene stove. He went out to buy cigarettes and never came back. She waited for him for weeks and finally went back to Madras with Anjolie and a bag of dirty clothes.

Anjolie grew up with her mother in a tiny flat in Tiruvanmayur from where you could see the sea and into the neighbour's house. With a pair of beautiful eyes and a few dozen French words up her sleeve, her mother worked as a tourist guide to Europeans who came to India looking for elephants on the streets. She made most of her money from tips and went to Thomas Cook to exchange them for rupees. She bought Anjolie no toys but taught her yoga at the age of twelve and gave her wings to fly.

Anjolie would wake up at the crack of dawn and practise yoga on the terrace. Then she would take two buses to college and another one to the Alliance. She would come back home and cook dinner for two. After dinner, her mum would fall asleep on the crumbling sofa and she would retire to the bedroom of their one-bedroom flat as insomniac as Proust. Lying on a mattress on the mosaic floor, her head leaning against the reverberating wall, she spent her nights reading Rimbaud, Baudelaire, Flaubert, Jarry and Artaud.

She got a scholarship to study at the École des Beaux-Arts. Her mum gave her an old map of Paris and seventy-seven assorted French franc bills and kissed her goodbye at the airport. Anjolie settled into her window seat and after Madras had disappeared below her eyes, she pulled out *L'Etranger* from her handbag and began to read.

Maman died today. Or yesterday maybe, I don't know. I got a telegram from the home: Mother deceased. Funeral tomorrow. Faithfully yours. That doesn't mean anything. Maybe it was yesterday.

The École des Beaux-Arts was located just across from the Louvre, in the heart of Saint-Germain-des-Près, home to a menagerie of artists. Sauntering along the crooked, cobbled streets of the Latin Quarter, she made love instead of paintings and sculpted her mind like the Gates of Hell. And in her second year at the École, she met the New York based performance artist Marina Abromovic, who opened the door to a whole new world of art: performance art.

Performance art was live. There were no rules. It could be any situation that involved the four basic elements of time, space, the performer's body and a relationship between the performer and the audience. It was opposed to painting where the object constituted the work. Here the process constituted the work. It could not be bought or sold. It could be amusing, it could be horrifying but it had to be memorable.

Anjolie watched a video clip of *Lips of Thomas* – a 1975 Abromovic performance where the artist sliced her skin and carved a star into her stomach with a razor blade – and imagined using her own body as a medium for her work. Marina's words kept ringing in her ears. 'In normal life, if I cut myself I cry like a baby, but in a performance, pain is not an issue. It's all about removing the fear of pain by staging the pain in front of an audience, going through the pain in front of spectators and turning it into something else.' You could explore the limits of the body, Anjolie realized, and the possibilities of the mind. During a performance, you could push your body to extremes and somehow find the energy to do so. Pain was a good door to another state of consciousness.

Anjolie crossed over to another state of consciousness at the age of twenty-three as she restaged *Lips of Thomas*. Waiting at the wings before the performance, she had butterflies in her stomach. They were beating their wings like the crows that Van Gogh painted before he died. She didn't know if she could go through with it; she wanted to call it off and escape into the painting with the restless crows but the moment she stepped on stage and looked at the audience, she found the power to do it. She thought later that this power had been trapped inside her belly all these years, waiting to come into the spotlight.

She stood naked in front of the audience, carved a star into her stomach with a razor blade and watched the blood trickle over her groin. It was meditative, it was calming and it was not painful. She had found a new person inside her that she never knew existed.

The Anjolie off stage was very different from the Anjolie on stage. That Anjolie was fragile like glass on a window pane before the neighbour's ball strikes, she was soft like a petal before it falls off a rose. She cried, she laughed, sometimes coyly at her own pieces.

It was that Anjolie who flew back to meet her mother and ended up meeting a handsome young scientist on the flight. They sat next to each other, she in her window seat looking at the shrinking Parisian lights, he in the aisle seat gazing past her at the expanding sky. As the plane soared above a million street cafés with invisible people clustered around carafes, Anjolie pulled out her boarding pass that lay between page seventy-two and seventy-three of *Le Tour du Monde en 80 Jours* and he unfurled an omnibus edition of *The Hitchhiker's Guide to the Galaxy*.

So he's a galactic voyager, Anjolie thought; she's drop dead gorgeous, Neel thought and did something he had never done before. He flirted. He told her he would take her to a restaurant at the end of the world and asked for her phone number. She laughed and wrote it down on a paper napkin.

He called her a week later and took her to Fisherman's Cove. It was not at the end of the world, but after all the Bloody Marys and fish, the conversations about life, the universe and everything beyond, when they stood up to leave, it felt like the end of the world. Three months later, she married him, her curly-haired genius with dark eyes and an answer to everything. She moved back to Madras and went back to her first love: painting. She painted the ocean, she painted the sky and she painted her toes, her feet, her calves and her thighs as she saw them through her eyes.

Anjolie sat in the lotus pose and mixed three shades of brown with her brush, observing the curve of her calf muscles. She sat in that position for six-and-a-half hours and painted. She stretched out one leg and then the other and put her brush down.

It was three o'clock. She went into the kitchen and poured herself an orange juice and dropped two cubes of ice into it. She sat in the balcony with her glass and looked at the trees through the grills. It was hot. The sun was burning through the sky. She sipped the cold juice and as her lips touched the rim of the glass, she thought of *him*. He must be at home, writing something. She pictured him in his house writing in a giant notepad, writing a song to serenade her with; she pictured him in his house on a chair by the window, and then she pictured his wife. Suddenly there was mist everywhere – between the trees and sunlight, between the grills and the patch of sky – and everything went out of shape. The grill was crooked, the tree was bent, the sunlight was cloudy. When she put down the glass, the tree straightened up, the grills aligned themselves and the sun shone bright as only a Chennai sun could shine.

4

It was a bright yellow afternoon in February. It had been over a year since I moved back to this blazing city with a new-fangled name. Someone had decided to change its name while I was away in London and my poor old city had lost its name like I had when I was a little girl.

I was walking home for lunch after spending all morning at the clinic and when I pushed the gate open and went inside, who should be standing in the doorway but Sid.

I froze.

I could see that he was utterly amused by the expression on my face. I felt like I was in a dream and I would wake up any minute and find myself in bed listening to the murmur of the air-conditioner.

'Good afternoon, doc,' said Sid, grinning. 'I saw the shining golden nameplate outside and I thought I'd drop in and see if the doctor was in.'

'Why?' I asked, beaming. 'Do you need treatment?'

'Special treatment.'

'That you always got.'

'I'm not too sure I'll still get that. After all, it's been more than ten years.'

It had been more than ten years since the day he left for Calcutta, looking like a soldier going to war, leaving me with a horrible feeling in my belly that I would never see him again. And now here he was in flesh and blood, looking like a million bucks.

'And you look even prettier,' he said, reading my thoughts. 'But what's with the sari and all, doc? You look like a good Brahmin girl, but that doesn't fool me.'

He had never seen me in a sari before. I had been wearing them ever since I started practising in Madras, and with that and my untamed hair rolled up in a knot at the nape of my neck, I must have looked altered. We went inside the house and I laid the table for two and brought out the spread that the cook had made: vatha kuzhambu, lemon rasam, keera kootu and avial, with heaps of rice and potato roast.

'I don't know about you but I'm starved,' I said.

'Me too,' he said, his eyes twinkling, his mind forever interpreting words like poems.

We sat down to eat and through that delightfully long lunch we caught up on the last ten years. I told him about life in London and about moving back to an empty home. I told him about Shanti and all that transpired between us; she was a big part of my life during those General Hospital days. I told him about Zubeida and Megha, Tulsi and Anjolie, Pooja and Leela. He told me he had lost his mother and that his father was living in Auroville making solar panels. He had travelled all over the world, writing for the *Lonely Planet*, and now he was back in India to write a travelogue. Back to the basics, he said. Back to your roots, I said. His long hair was now in a crew cut and he looked as delectable as the meal before us. I wanted to ask him if he was seeing someone but I didn't want to be the first to bring that up. And then he read my mind once again.

'A beautiful girl like you wouldn't be alone, would she?'

'She would,' I said, feeling like a girl again, something I hadn't felt in a long, long time. I was tired of being the grown up, the woman well above her years who was fixing broken hearts and parts.

'That makes two of us,' he said.

I looked at the time. Three hours had gone by and yet it felt like I had just walked through the gate and set my eyes on him. Time always had a mind of its own when Sid was around. I was late for my first afternoon appointment.

'I have to rush,' I said.

'That makes two of us.'

He looked into my eyes and my heart ticked away like a wall clock in the dead of night. That's the problem when you're in conversation with a writer and you're a voracious reader. They talk like dialogues in a novel and you're left reading between the lines. Did he mean that we have to rush into this like we rushed into it years ago when we were in our twenties and living on dreams? Or did he simply have to go?

But he didn't get up. He was stretched out cheerfully on the sofa beside me and I wanted to hold his face and feel his crew cut against my fingers.

'Stay right there,' I said. 'I'll be back in a few hours.'

'I have a train to catch but I'll be back.'

'When?'

'The weekend after next. Or is the doctor on call on weekends too?'

'Only for special treatments. And this time can I have a number or something or will you disappear on me again?'

'I wasn't the one who disappeared the last time, remember? I just went onto my next assignment. You came to visit me and said you can't go on like this and you left the country without a forwarding address.'

Yes, indeed I did. I couldn't bear to see him go, so I came up with the big London plan and left. And now I wanted to fall into his arms again. I wanted to slide my hand under his shirt and feel those forgotten biceps. I wanted to put my head on his shoulder and burst into tears. Instead, I bunched up my hair in a knot, adjusted the pleats of my sari and walked out of the house.

—

The water feels like drops of lead, thought Tulsi, standing under the shower. She lathered herself with Pears soap and the glycerine scent brought back memories of a summer several years ago when she was a little girl who spent her afternoons reading *The Secret Seven* in the plastic tub in her grandmother's house. She imagined meeting the neighbourhood children in the shed with admission by password only, guzzling down lemonade and solving mysteries. Her brother Ram, who was four years older than her, would be head of the society, she decided. He would make the rules and delegate tasks and this time he could implement them on children other than her. She told him about her idea and soon they started a secret society. It included three of her cousins and a neighbourhood boy. They called themselves 'The Secret Six' and went about solving imaginary crimes all summer. Her brother took his responsibilities very seriously, she remembered, laughing as she lathered her neck. How she

missed him! He went to New York to study and ended up
staying on. He married an American girl and they made
a trip to India every few years with their three kids. She
adored her nieces and her nephew, who looked just like her
brother when he was a little boy. How she missed him, the
little boy who used to be her brother. Now he was all grown
up and he still took his responsibilities very seriously.

Her cousins were all grown up too, but when they were
little they spent every summer vacation at their grandmother's
house. They would play all day and when one of them fell
down and scraped a knee, the others would crowd around
while their grandfather cleaned the wound with cotton and
dressed it with a flesh-coloured Band-Aid with bright pink
holes in the centre.

It's the intricacies that matter, thought Tulsi, remembering
the bright pink dots. She looked at the petal patterns on the
bathroom tiles. Was it a rose or a cabbage with open leaves?
She lathered her thighs, her calves and her feet, making sure
to reach between her toes. And then the soap slid from her
fingers like her husband had an hour ago.

She had lain in bed after making love, her bottom thrust
over a heap of pillows, her legs raised and her toes pointing
to the ceiling. Swim, you little fish, she said to a thousand
sperms in her vagina, to a thousand monsters in her head;
swim down and gobble up the egg. Dhruv jumped out of
bed and told her to stop, to stop all the leg lifting and toe
pointing, to stop counting time, to stop counting days as if
the world revolved around her menstrual calendar. Stop it,
he told her and stormed out of the room. Tulsi didn't stop.
She waited a whole twenty minutes before bringing her legs
down and going in to shower. Then the soap slid from her
fingers and she felt light and frothy.

She stepped out of the shower and wrapped a towel around her head. It soaked up the water from her hair like a sponge. She had read that sponges of a certain species release their eggs and sperm on the same night and fertilize each other in the water. If she were a sponge, she would do just that. She pulled out a red t-shirt from her cupboard and wore it over a pair of jeans. Her short brown hair was already dry and she tucked it behind her ears and reeled into the living room. She would wrap herself around Dhruv and tell him he was right, that she was obsessing over the issue of not having an issue, and they would laugh and think about that night on the Trivandrum Mail.

They were on their way to spend a long weekend by the Arabian Sea and they sat next to each other, doing the Sunday crossword. When she went to sleep on the top berth, Dhruv kissed her goodnight and started to read. An old man who had been watching them for some time asked him, 'Do you have any issues?' Dhruv smiled and said, 'No, sir, no issues! We've been married a good seven years and we've had no issues!' The old man was asking if they had offspring and Dhruv was referring to a matter in dispute, knowing full well what the old man had meant.

Sometimes nosey old women would ask Tulsi if there was any 'good news' and she would reply, 'Yes, aunty! I won ten Ad Club awards!' Dhruv and she would laugh about it when they were alone.

But where was he now?

She saw a yellow Post-it note on the door. *I don't care if we ever have a baby*, it said in blue ink, *but I don't want to lose my baby in the process. D.*

She wanted to leap into his arms but where was he? He must have gone for a run. He ran only when he was angry or confused, and considering he was rarely angry or confused, he ran very little. And still he had the body of a runner. He would run his anger away and come back home.

But it wasn't anger that Dhruv was running away as he ran down Cenotaph Lane and took a right on TTK Road. It wasn't anger he was running away as he ran past the red and green lights and crossed Chamiers Road. It wasn't anger he was running away as he passed the petrol pump and ran into Boat Club Road. It was confusion.

Why had Anjolie kissed him like that? When he had moved his face forward to kiss her, she moved her face back and looked at him looking at her, and for three seconds they kept staring into each other's eyes and for the life of him he didn't know what her eyes were saying. Then when he was about to move his face away, she kissed him quickly, her lips pulling his lower lip and then letting go.

He had met her a few weeks ago at a friend's studio. He and the boys were jamming and there was a knock on the door followed by the entry of the most beautiful woman he had ever seen. She was looking for a trumpet player, she said. None of them played the trumpet, though they all immediately wished they did.

'I don't know a trumpet player,' said Dhruv, 'but we play other instruments.'

'I can see that,' she said and flashed a voluptuous smile at them.

'What do you need a trumpet player for?' Dhruv asked.

'I'm choreographing a piece that involves a trumpet being played in the background.'

'I can play the guitar if that helps,' he said with a sheepish grin.

She laughed. She stayed back and heard them play. It

became darker, the air became smokier and she looked surreal under the studio lights. Then she got up and said that she hadn't had such a great time in years, and turned to leave.

Dhruv walked her to her car.

'So you're a dancer?' he asked.

'No,' she said, 'I'm a performance artist. Rather, I was. Now I'm just an artist.'

He had heard about performance art but he had never met a performance artist before.

She told him about the years she had spent in Paris and about her best performances in New York and Amsterdam. She told him about her scorpion piece at the Guggenheim.

When he thought of how she must have cut herself on stage, he felt a strange tingle in his hands, like a tickle, like he had to pick her up then and there or she might fall down. This is crazy, he said finally, putting his hands in his pockets. He didn't pick her up – not that day – he picked up his phone three days later and dialled her number.

They met at Amethyst. They sat in the verandah of the old colonial villa and sipped endless cups of espresso. It seemed as if the whole world was in soft focus while she placed an elbow on the table and laughed. He couldn't stop himself that day; he was on a roll.

Dhruv kept thinking about her after that. Since the day he turned around and saw Tulsi looking at his ass, he hadn't thought of anyone else. But now he thought about Anjolie. She crept into his head when he least expected it, like this afternoon with Tulsi.

She had come back to the studio yesterday – to hear them play, she told the boys – and confessed to him when he walked her to the car that she had come to see him. She got into her car, closed the door and rolled down the window with a smile. When he leaned over to kiss her, she tilted her head back and looked into his eyes, and just when he was about to move his head away, she kissed him. That little kiss changed everything.

Now he imagined Anjolie's body under the tight parrot-green blouse she had been wearing; he imagined what her breasts would feel like under his palms – soft like clouds, he decided – and he imagined kissing her again.

He slowed down and stopped to stretch by the side of the empty road. The air was motionless and warm. He looked at the leaves on a tree. They hung unmoving under the damp evening sun. This leaf looks odd, he thought, focusing on a bright green spot. It looked so odd that it didn't look like a leaf at all. As he moved away, the leaf seemed to move closer to him and that was when he saw her: the parrot-green praying mantis camouflaged on the leaf. She was looking at him with two dots for eyes and tilted her head when he stretched. Her forelimbs were folded in prayer. If anything were to wander within range of those forelimbs, they would snap shut. A male mantis approached her, flapping his wings and swaying his abdomen. He leapt onto her back and began to mate and she tore off his head. Dhruv walked his last round and then returned to the tree. The female mantis was still sitting on the leaf but the male mantis was gone; only his wings were left.

It was Sunday. There were few joggers on the road. A woman was pushing a stroller in which a gigantic white baby sat staring at the sky with blue eyes. Dhruv bought a pack of cigarettes on TTK Road and walked to his apartment on Cenotaph Lane, having found no answers. Instead, he had more questions.

He put his key into the keyhole. It slid into the hole, the

notches and grooves fitting into the hole naturally, as if this was where it was meant to be, inside this keyhole and none other. He turned the key and the door opened. Tulsi flew into his arms and kissed his cheeks.

'I'm sorry,' she said. 'I'm so sorry. I'm never putting my legs up in that ridiculous fashion again and from now on, we're not going to make love unless we really want to.'

They decided to go for a movie. They went to Sathyam Cinemas and got tickets for *Coyote Ugly*. As they sat next to each other, digging into the buttery popcorn, he thought of the male praying mantis.

Only his wings were left.

———

Anjolie held the parrot-green blouse to her face and inhaled before throwing it into the laundry basket. This is how she must have smelt for those three seconds before she kissed him. I smell like lilies, she said to herself, and kissed Neel awake from his Sunday afternoon nap.

She lay down next to him with her head on his shoulder. The evening sunlight formed shadows through the window and the grills looked like charcoal paintings on the marble floor. This is paramount, she thought, this moment. The floor was filled with shadows, her husband's naked arms were around her body, she was thinking of somebody else and the parrot-green blouse was inside the laundry basket. And then, slowly, ever so slowly, the charcoal patterns inched their way across the floor and disappeared.

Her cell-phone rang. Every time it rang, her heart rang with it like a hollow drum that had been struck. Would he call her today? He had to call her today or she would die from being struck again and again.

It was her mum.

'Hope you're not planning to visit today,' she screamed into the phone. 'I'm going to Kapaleeshwarar kovil.'

Her mother spent all her time praying. She had transformed Anjolie's old room into a shrine. She had bought an assortment of technicolour gods – Krishnas, Ramas, Ganeshas and a handful of goddesses on bright pink lotuses – and placed them at strategic positions on the bookshelf.

But when Anjolie was a child, things were very different. Her mother would spend all Sunday indoors smelling like a skunk and watching the world from her window. Her downstairs neighbours would go to the beach and come back with peanuts stuffed into newspaper cones. Her upstairs neighbours would go to the temple and come back with broken coconuts. Anjolie would shake her mother and say, 'Take me to the beach, ma, take me to the temple! Everybody goes somewhere on Sunday.' But her mother would not budge.

'Take me somewhere,' she said to Neel, still lying on his shoulder. 'Take me somewhere and don't tell me where.'

He got out of bed and put on a t-shirt over his shorts. She tossed her hair back and straightened her skirt. They got into the car and drove off. They crossed the Adyar bridge. They drove past the Theosophical Society, past the left turn to Elliot's beach, past Maharaja, past her childhood home in Tiruvanmayur. Now they were on ECR Road. She rolled down the window and let the wind play with her hair. Houses flew past like paper planes and between the houses was a glimpse of the sea. It was a speck of blue left to the imagination to extend and her imagination extended it, blew it up like a rubber balloon on all sides and filled it with weightless air till it was blue, blue, blue everywhere.

They drove past the drive-in theatre where nobody drove in, past the artist's village which wasn't a village, past the crocodile bank where crocodiles posed for curious onlookers with their jaws wide open; they drove past Fisherman's Cove, Silver Sands and Golden Sun and then he took a left where the road forked into two.

'Now you have a beach and a temple in the same place,' Neel said and parked the car outside the Mahabalipuram Shore Temple.

She squeezed his hand. They walked around the temple that was built over a thousand years ago and rescued from the sea. They went to the seashore and ate peanuts on the sand. He bought her a bracelet made of seashells and a batik skirt that smelt of Goa. They went to the Moonraker restaurant where they drank beer and talked. It was hot, they said, it was really hot. The weather had suddenly changed. It was as if April was announcing its arrival in the third week of March on the terrace of Moonraker.

The food arrived. It was an enormous seafood fare that was hotter than the weather. They dug into the masala fish with their fingers and poured prawn gravy over rice. And then her phone beeped. She had received a message.

I saw a praying mantis today, it said. *And it looked like you.*

Suddenly the fish tasted delicious. She squeezed more lemon over it and bit into it. It was crisp and juicy and between the masala and lemon, she could taste the sea.

I drove past seven thousand crocodiles without seeing them, she typed, *and they all looked like you.*

When Sid came back on Saturday morning like he had promised, I thought the world had expanded with the universe and Mylapore had shrunk to the size of a doorknob. He was holding two tickets in his hand and I knew it was not the destination that mattered; it was what he held in the palm of his spacious hand and how he held it, looking at me with absolute confidence that he had done the perfect thing.

'Just what the doctor ordered,' he said and slipped the tickets into my hands.

I shut the door and fell into his arms and then we were laughing, kissing, making up for the decade in between when the world had continued as usual in circles around the sun.

And so we went on the first of our glorious weekends, and I came home three days later with the smell of the sea lingering in my hair. Everything took on new meaning and everything lost meaning at the same time; my heart had risen like the sun over a chagrined sea and I could feel the end of one heartbeat and the beginning of the next.

I threw myself into my work with renewed energy and I started seeing patients round the clock, plunging myself into their lives, lives which were somehow more penetrable than mine. When I was at home, I read to overcome the silence. Lewis Carroll, George Orwell, T.S. Eliot, Rabindranath Tagore, Aldous Huxley, Thomas Hardy, Virginia Woolf. I reread the works of Tennessee Williams and suddenly, one side of my brain that had been dead all these years screamed for more and all the reading in the world would not assuage it. So one day, I went to my desk by the window, opened a word file and began to write.

That is how I began this book. It was as if it had to be written to save me from myself. Slowly, the women from my practice began to appear in my head. The voluptuous Zubeida who was yearning for a girl, the emaciated Megha who had to have a boy, Anjolie and Tulsi who loved the same man. And then, by some stroke of fortune or misfortune, something in my heart paired Leela and Pooja together like sisters of an impending doom. I did not know what it was then, all I knew was that I had to tell their stories. As I wrote, life took on a deeper significance, and as I watched their stories unfold before my eyes, I discovered the meanings hidden in things, and with that I pacified my relentless heart.

5

Leela sat at her desk wearing a bright orange sweater over her yellow maternity dress which stretched out to accommodate the foetus that was now amply developed for life outside her uterus. It was cold. It was always cold inside her office and if she looked through the window at the radiating sun, it was hard to believe that it was her world outside, that it was her tropical city that lay on the thermal equator.

The office was half empty. Most of her colleagues were at Chepauk or in the canteen watching the three Test series between India and Australia. After losing the first test miserably in Mumbai, India had gone on to beat the Australians hollow in Kolkata when V.V.S. Laxman scored a formidable 281 in the second innings, and now, buoyed by their historic performance at Eden Gardens, the Indian team was playing the third and crucial Test in Chennai.

She got back to the task at hand, the application that she was designing for JP Morgan. It was a loan calculator that would calculate the risk rate of a person applying for a loan.

If she were to calculate her risk rate, it would be zero. She had never put anything in jeopardy her whole life, she had always played it safe.

The phone rang. It was Srinivasan – her husband, not her father. He was calling to check on her like he had done every day in this last trimester. They discussed baby names over the phone and shortlisted a few but his mother was intent on naming her after *her* mother and Leela couldn't think of a baby called Amruthavalli coming into the world in the twenty-first century. As it was, her son was called Sadasivam after some great-grandfather or other but that she had been willing to accept because he was born in the twentieth century albeit the fag end of it. But to call her daughter Amruthavalli was criminal. She hung up and looked at the Java codes she had written on the computer screen. The programming language was initially called Oak after an oak tree that stood outside the designer's office, and later went by the name Green, and was finally renamed Java from a list of random words. Why not choose her baby's name from a list of random words? Why did it have to be the name of a goddess? She would call her baby Java, she thought fondly, after her favourite language, and they would communicate with a syntax of their own, their own set of rules that would define what is correct and what is not.

———

The day after she went to see *Dil Chahta Hai* with Anu, the day Sunil said he would come home, Pooja woke up bright and early, though she had hardly slept all night, and went into the bathroom to shave her legs. That was the first thing she did, even before squeezing out the fat tube of toothpaste onto her skinny brush. She lathered her legs with soap and gently ran the razor across her legs, and when her legs were smooth, she felt an urge to cut herself.

She made a neat straight line along her shin. The blood popped out in little drops and dribbled down to her ankle. Just then the doorbell rang and she ran into the living room in her shorts and her mother said, 'Darling! You've cut yourself while shaving again. Why don't you just wax next time?' But it was only the milkman who had come for his money.

She went back to the bathroom. What a waste of blood, she thought; it all went down the drain. She towelled herself dry and put on her lucky jeans. It wouldn't be good to expose her mutilated leg to Sunil. She blow-dried her curls away and sat on her bed until her mother called her for breakfast. Hot aloo parathas were heaped on a plate and set in the middle of the dining table. She served herself one and told her mother she would eat in her room while studying. Once in her room, she mashed the paratha to pulp and flushed it down the toilet.

It felt like days had elapsed while she sat in her room with a geography book spread across her lap, waiting for Sunil, and then her mother called her for lunch. This time it wouldn't be easy to get away. She sat at the table and picked at her food and finally managed to stomach a few spoonfuls of rice. Then she went back to her room and waited until evening, imagining the grains of rice turn into stone. And when her mother called her for dinner, she lost her mind.

It was like losing your way back home. She was sitting at the table, staring at her plate. The peas were bright green, the gravy was deep red, and above her head the ceiling was floating like a giant cloud. When she looked at her parents sitting right in front of her, they looked right through her.

It was as if she was made of glass and they were looking at the Matisse imitation hanging on a two-inch nail on the wall behind her. She could see the painting too, even though it was behind her, and she could see the backs of her parents' heads – her mother's long silky hair tied up in a knot, her father's salt-and-pepper locks cropped above his neck, the lamp dangling between them. And then it was blank, three dots left to the imagination to fill as she sank lower and lower into her chair and the walls evaporated into the distance.

The next thing she knew, she was lying in a psychiatrist's couch and he gave her little white pills and taught her how to breathe. Her father held her hand when she walked out of the door and when they were back home, her mother popped two little pills into her mouth. She slept like a baby that night, making up for all the sleepless nights when she had lain in bed staring at the moon through her window. When she woke up the next morning, the sun looked like a dirty tennis ball. It was millions of miles away and she realized she would never hold it in her hand and play again.

Once that realization dawned on her, she began to rise inch by inch over the coming weeks, even studying with deep concentration at times, and wrote her board exams. She was over three months pregnant and she had to hide her belly behind baggy pants. She hadn't meant to wait this long; in fact, during her gynaecologist's appointment in January, she wanted to do it right away but the doc had asked her to take some tests and come back and she had taken them, but before she could go back, she had a nervous breakdown.

And now the sun caved in like a grotto around her and the deep dark shadow around her belly seemed to be getting the better of her. Pooja took deep breaths like the psychiatrist had demonstrated. Her belly rose high as she breathed in till the count of twelve and then she imagined all the panic leaving her body as she breathed out through her mouth. She repeated the exercise twenty-one times like he had said and the last time she imagined they were her birthday candles – all seventeen of them – that she was blowing out.

She opened the pregnancy book she had borrowed from the library. Your baby is the size of a lemon now, she read. He can squint, frown, grimace and pee. If you're having an ultrasound today, you can even catch him sucking his thumb.

She went to the section on abortion. She found out that they would have to do a D&E now that she was in her second trimester. Instead of the loop-shaped knife used in the usual D&C abortions, a pair of forceps is inserted in the womb to grasp the foetus. The teeth of the forceps twist and tear the bones until the foetus is totally dismembered and expelled.

Like a firecracker, Pooja thought, shutting the book and hiding it under her pillow. It would tear apart and come out with a bang.

6

Sunday evening by the window. The verandah is filled with potted plants: hibiscus, ixora, jacobina, catharanthus, cryptanthus and croton. And in the middle is a large cane-bottom easy chair that belonged to my grandfather. I had the rosewood edges scraped and polished and the hand-woven cane replaced. When I was a little girl I would climb up the back of the chair and slide down the long cane seat, landing at the edge. Now I fill the chair.

The fan hums above my head. Trailing stems of money plant are entwined around the grills and the heart-shaped leaves flutter rhythmically in the wind. Between the grill and the greenish-yellow leaves is the street laid out like an operating table under the evening sun.

Yesterday I performed a hysterectomy on a twenty-five-year-old girl. She had ovarian cancer. Her hair had fallen from the chemo and she looked freshly waxed from head to toe but she had a smile on her face before going under anaesthesia. I am going to live, she must have said to herself before the needle jabbed her veins. My hair will grow back. I won't have any children but I am going to live.

I made a vertical incision in her lower abdomen, cutting through the skin and connective tissue, and removed her uterus, ovaries and Fallopian tubes. Looking at her open young body lying motionless under my gloved hands, I felt that I was removing her womanhood, that I was robbing her of her womb before she had even made love for the first time. But now I realize I was wrong; I could remove it all and she would still be a woman, a living, breathing, thinking woman, because we are what we are inside our heads and not inside our bodies.

The sun has begun to fade. Mum calls from California and says that she has found a cardiologist in San Diego. Why, I ask her, is something wrong with your heart? No, silly girl, she says, it's for you. She never gives up, my dear mother. You need a man, she says. You need someone to talk to at the end of the day. And then she whispers into the phone, you need to have sex. At your age, she begins, your father and I… I get the picture, ma, I say quickly. I have a man in my life, I want to say but I can't bring myself to. What do I tell her? That I love someone and he loves me back but he's not the marrying kind? You've met him, ma, I imagine myself saying. His name is Sid. He travels in and out of my life as he pleases but we have great sex. Sometimes I think it's because we're not married, we don't live together and bring home every nitty-gritty life throws at us. Instead, we make sure we smell good and we laugh and we put our best faces forward. But I don't tell her a thing.

Mum says goodbye and hands the phone to Maya. I tell her about Sid. She listens disapprovingly and tells me I should leave him if he's not willing to make a commitment. But he's made a commitment, I tell her, to himself. Just as I have to myself. Isn't that enough? I can picture her shaking her head at the other end but she doesn't say a word. Suddenly the years between us seem as wide as the seas that separate us. And yet we come from the same womb, developing eyes, ears and a heart inside the same home before we took our first breath.

On her first day at school, she told me once, mum was in the hospital giving birth to me. Dad was late picking her up because he was busy looking at me. And when she went to the hospital with tears running down her cheeks, she looked at my baby face and wanted to squash it. Since she couldn't, she took it upon herself to make my life difficult. When I was three, she was almost seven and she'd tell me she was going to the cinema with mum and dad but that I wasn't going. Nee cinemaku kadayadhu, she'd say with authority. Undu sollu, Maya, I'd reply with equal servitude. Tell me I'm going too. Oh please, please tell me, Maya! Then get me a glass of water, she'd say, stretching herself on the sofa. In a glass glass, she'd spell out as I wobbled into the kitchen. And put some ice in it!

I couldn't figure out that mum and dad were not going to leave me alone in the house and go to the cinema with Maya. I believed her. I believed everything Maya said. When she told me that cats have nine lives and we have two, I believed her, and when she said that little girls who disobey their big sisters are sent away to a hostel, I believed her then too. But as the years went by, she became mellow. She would draw my science diagrams and teach me geometry. She would crawl into my bed at night and tell me secrets till I fell asleep. Soon I caught up with her in height and we shared clothes, chains, bangles and dreams. I don't miss Maya, not any

more, but on a day when I've done something remarkable at
work, performed a particularly skilful surgery, for instance,
I imagine telling Maya all about it, describing it to her in
great detail, knowing full well that she will understand even
though she has never studied medicine.

I put down the phone and open a book. A postcard brings
me back to my world. Sid sent it to me from Tibet. *Thinking
of you*, it says in large flamboyant letters behind a picture
of the Jokhang temple. It's tucked between the pages of
Dialogues Concerning the Two Chief World Systems. What is very
hard for us to understand is very easy for nature to perform,
says Galileo on that page. Sometimes I think that they are
the gods, the Galileos and Darwins of this world, but people
pray to dead ones. While the universe grows a day older and
galaxies inch away from each other, we evolve as a human
race. My niece wrote to me yesterday. Malu chitti, she types
from halfway across the world, when will you visit us? She
is six years old. When my grandmother died at the age of
eighty-eight, she still couldn't read or write. And yet, no
matter how much we evolve, we are far from discovering the
mysteries of life. Take, for instance, the human body. There
are over a hundred trillion cells inside the body and each
one has its own function. How they perform harmoniously,
executing millions of tasks without colliding into each other,
is a mystery in itself and how they came into being, slowly
dividing and replicating themselves from one original cell,
is an even greater mystery.

It is dark outside. The phone rings. It's the clinic
calling to tell me that two women have gone into labour
simultaneously. Internal examinations have been performed,
foetal heartbeats monitored, and now they are fully dilated
and ready for delivery. I put down my book, thinking of

Galileo's words. What is very hard for us to understand is very easy for nature to perform. I change into a sari, switch off the lights and leave in the darkness.

———

She got the sudden feeling that her waist was stuffed with rags, her hands were stuffed with rags and she had no elbows. Her legs had disappeared underneath her long trailing underskirt. Her face seemed to be carved out of wood with black eyes painted on it. Megha felt like one of the colourful string puppets she had seen in Udaipur when she was little. She felt like she had been dancing to the tunes of the ghungru for a thousand years and now she just wanted to stop. Her thighs ached, her calves ached, her feet ached. She wanted to put up her invisible feet and fold herself into a wooden box and sleep with the other puppets.

She pulled the end of her sari over her enormous belly and tucked it around her waist. Underneath her sari, her cervix was softening, ripening ever so slowly, without her knowing. She took out the vegetable basket and began to shell the peas by snapping off the ends of the pods. Her five-year-old daughter came running into the kitchen with tears in her eyes and a bruise on her knee.

'I told you not to run so much,' she said, picking her up.

'Rahul made me chase him and chase him and said that if I caught him, I could do whatever I want,' the little girl said, talking of her cousin who was three years older than her.

'You can't do whatever you want; anyway, Rahul is not the one to give you permission.'

'He said, I wear pants so I can tell you what to do.'

'You can wear pants too, if you want, Barkha beti.'

'Mama, will you buy me a pair of pants?'

'As soon as papa comes home, we'll ask him, okay?'

'Mama, I have a better idea!'

'What is it, jaan?'

'Why don't *you* wear pants? Then you won't have to ask papa!'

Megha cleaned her daughter's knee with a swab of cotton wool and imagined herself in pants. She would look like an ass, she thought; a grey-dun ass with a hind leg ready to kick. She had never worn pants before but she had seen girls wear them: in the supermarket, in the mithai shop, in the movie theatre and in the movies themselves.

She kissed her daughter's knee. The girl stopped crying and ran into the garden to catch her cousin and tell him that she would be wearing pants too. Megha wanted to tell her that she didn't have to catch him, she didn't have to wear pants, she didn't have to *do* something to do what she wanted to do.

Slowly the light began to fade and she looked out of the window. Outside, it was still bright enough to see. She saw a squirrel perched on a coconut tree. She saw a dark blue butterfly with orange wings. The sun was slowly disappearing under the horizon, moving away from the world inch by inch, bathing every creature in darkness. But it was the world that was moving away, *her* world that was moving away from the sun, and soon she would be plunged into darkness.

She switched on the lamp. Suddenly she felt as though she was wearing a belt around her lower back and abdomen, as though she was wearing pants and a tight belt was squeezing her oversized belly. Her teeth were numb, the colours in the kitchen were getting brighter. Her uterine muscles were contracting and her cervix was expanding without her knowledge, expanding like a millipede at the edge of the universe, slowly moving its feet one by one on both sides of its body until it sprung back and shut itself into a tight coil.

The house was filled with people. Her husband had come back home from work, her father-in-law was sitting on the sofa, her mother-in-law had descended from her bedroom and her sister-in-law was telling her that she would have a boy this time because her stomach drooped all the way down. Megha held onto that drooping belly for dear life and squeezed into the car and they all drove to the hospital.

———

A kilometre away, a kilometre as the crow flies from Purasawalkam, over the half-abandoned Dasaprakash hotel, over the Museum Theatre where a Shakespearean play was in its third act, over the Cosmopolitan Club where young men played billiards around bottles of beer, over the loud minarets of the Wallajah mosque, in a small apartment with green windows and peeling paint, Zubeida's water broke.

'Don't have a bath or sex after your water breaks,' her doctor had said. Her husband had come home and they were just about to have sex. Instead, they were having a baby. He ran into the street to call an auto-rickshaw and she ran into the bedroom to pack her dog-eared copy of *To Kill a Mockingbird* with some clothes and a toothbrush.

Her contractions were ten minutes apart. It was like the minute hand of the Royapettah Clock Tower if it were to jump from odd number to odd number. Then they became stronger and more rhythmic, pulling and tightening and slowly expanding throughout her uterus, onto her back and groin.

The auto-rickshaw arrived and they left the apartment.

A rat ran in front of her and her sons followed her down the narrow staircase. Her burqa metamorphosed into a queer looking gypsy coat and she felt like the Pied Piper of Hamelin; her sons were running behind her, there was music in the air and she had a sinking feeling in the pit of her stomach that they would all drown with her.

What if it wasn't a girl?

It had been her dream, since she was a child playing mother to her doll, to have a daughter and tell her the things that nobody had told her. What happens to a swallowed seed? Do birds sleep at night? Does a spider get caught in its own web?

The rutted ride to the clinic came to an end with a thud. Her husband pulled out his tattered wallet to pay the driver, who grabbed the fifty-rupee note and shoved it into his khaki pocket. She looked through the wrought iron gates of the clinic and wondered what awaited her inside. She wanted to get into bed and sleep – sleep between contractions, sleep between thoughts – she wanted to sleep and sleep and wake up to a beautiful dream.

I knew Megha could feel the shape of the baby; she could feel herself sitting on its head as it moved down. I told her to blow gently and reach down and touch the baby's head, then breathe the baby out like a bubble.

Her skinny, anaemic body wouldn't stand another pregnancy. This was the last one. Outside, her husband waited with his parents who were eager to see the grandson who would carry the family name 'Jhunjhunwala' for generations. In a corner of the waiting room, her daughters played rock-paper-scissors, biding their time before they could see their mum again.

Megha was making eye contact with the baby as it was coming out. I wondered what she was feeling at that moment when she saw her baby's eyes and didn't know if it was a boy or a girl. Either way, I thought, it would change her life forever. Then the little body slid out of her vagina and into my hands.

She was finally in the light.

I had known four months back that it would be a girl. I had seen the scan but I couldn't tell Megha because foetal sex determination is illegal in India. I had to let her hope and wait, hope and wait, and then see it for herself.

I cut the umbilical cord and watched her hold the baby, her face expressionless. I kissed her pale cheek and told her something to bring the blood back: that a girl was soft like roses, that she would be there for her mama till she faded away, that you could dress her up in pretty little frocks. Finally I told her that a girl could do anything a boy could do and then I rushed to the next room where Zubeida's baby was waiting to come out and see the light.

———

He was already moving down the birth canal and Zubeida was pushing with each contraction. His head began to recede – two steps forward, one step back – and a few pushes later, he was out. I lifted him onto her bare belly so that she could touch him. She had tears streaming down her face, tears of joy mingled with tears of pain.

The umbilical cord was still attached to the placenta and pulsating. It was not too late, I thought. I hadn't told the Jhunjhunwalas yet. I could cut the cord and then switch the babies before anyone found out. Of course the mothers would know but I didn't think either of them would protest. Once the babies were cleaned, all I had to do was switch the blankets. Then I could give peace to Megha and a childhood dream to Zubeida; I could give them the babies that belonged to them, but I didn't.

Who was I to change the story?

I left Zubeida alone with her baby boy. Soon she was surrounded by more boys: her husband, her sons, her brothers-in-law. Even her father was there. He brought her biryani from Samco in a cardboard box and she wolfed it down. She seemed to be trying to fill the void that had now formed inside her belly. But it had formed long before she married and became a mother; it had formed when her childhood ended and she went plunging thousands of feet into womanhood.

And now that she had reached the bottom, there was no other way to go but up.

7

It rained early in the morning, just enough to soothe the earth from the heat that had begun the night before. It would cool down for some time and then it would be hot and humid again. The weather would get hotter and hotter and in the middle of May you would feel it in your bones and know it couldn't get any hotter, and then it would rain, and then it would be terribly hot again.

Now it was raining.

Tulsi wanted to stay home. There was something wonderful about staying home on a Monday morning when it rained. She looked out of the window and saw the milkman on the street. He had finished dropping a packet of milk at every doorstep, he had finished his work for the day when the rest of the city was just waking up to drink coffee and go to work.

The maid had let herself in with her key. She could hear coffee brewing in the kitchen (or was it the sound of rain?). Dhruv was sleeping next to her like a little boy. She leaned against him and put her head on his shoulder. He woke up, a frown on his face. Then he looked out of the window and smiled.

'It's raining,' he said.

'I'm not going to work. Let's stay home and watch the rain.'

'I have to go out for a couple of hours,' he said and picked up his phone from the bedside table. He jumped into a pair of jeans and swept out of the room. Tulsi lay in bed listening to the rain. She felt an urge to get up and do something: write a book, paint a picture, change the world. She got up as Van Gogh would have got up to paint the sunflowers and went to the bathroom. She sat down on the toilet and looked between her thighs into the pot. There was a tiny spider floating in the water. She peed into the pot and the spider went under the water. Oh my god, she thought, I'm going to kill it. But the spider found its way up and began to crawl along the walls of the pot. She must drown the spider in the pot, she decided, for if she didn't kill it at that moment, it would climb out of the pot and build cobwebs on the ceiling and she would have to dust them away with the spider one day.

She got up and wore her panties. She didn't kill the spider. She couldn't. When it grew big and built its cobweb, she would kill it. It would have spun its silk and weaved its web and created its art on the wall. Only then would it be ready to die.

But what have *I* done, she wondered. I haven't created art. I haven't even created life. And what of that? Everyone made babies – where was the art in that? Every second, five babies were born into the world but how many great pieces of art were born?

She would make her cobweb before she died, she decided.

Yes, that is what she would do. Her heart was racing now, her pulse was beating like drumbeats in a song that she could finally hear. She tucked her night shirt into a pair of jeans and counted the hundred-rupee notes in her wallet.

'I'm going out,' she said, sauntering into the living room, but Dhruv had left already. The newspaper lay abandoned beside an empty coffee cup and the apartment smelt like rain.

She drove down TTK Road and turned into Cathedral Road. She drove past Stella Maris College and took a U-turn and parked the car. There it was: the little stationary shop behind the chaat-seller. Tulsi opened her big black umbrella and heard the rain beating above her head (or was it her heart?). She crossed the street and stepped into the stationary shop. Suddenly it was as if all the other shops had shut, as if time had stopped and people were frozen in the April sun; cars had stopped to a soundless halt, and autos and scooters looked like listless toys. She picked up paints. She picked up canvasses. She picked up more paints. She paid the bill and stepped out of the shop with her umbrella and an enormous bag. Only then did people start to move again. Leaves began to rustle. Cars raced by, scooters flew past, buses swam through the humidity and people seemed to be walking faster to catch up with time.

When she finally reached home, she went straight to the guest bedroom. She separated the twin beds, moving each one against a wall, and set up the easel in the middle of the room. She put the paints on the bedside table. The canvas looked like a virgin, waiting for her touch.

Should I, should I touch the canvas?

Van Gogh described drawing as the act of working one's way through the invisible wall of iron that seems to lie between what one feels and what one can do. And how is one to get through this wall? One must undermine the wall, he says, and file one's way through slowly and patiently.

As the late morning opened up into afternoon and the grass became brighter and the leaves wider, Tulsi filed her way through the invisible wall. She worked until she couldn't breathe, until she couldn't see, and dropped to the floor with a bottle of paint. The glass broke on the mosaic floor and the paint dripped to the floor, silently writing its own story.

Then it started to fade. The grass faded. The leaves faded. The sky faded with the sun and she heard the clock on the table, beating with every second and throbbing inside her head. She grabbed it, put it into the drawer and shut it tight. Now it was silent. She lay on the floor and looked at the ceiling. The fan lay motionless. It was thirty-six degrees and she had forgotten to turn the fan on. Her hand touched the fallen paint and it felt syrupy against her wrist. She closed her eyes and listened to her heartbeat. It sounded like footsteps, tiny little footsteps walking for the first time. How she longed to hear those baby feet, to touch those baby thighs! They would grow bigger and bigger with each passing day, with each passing year, and then, as if she were turning a page in a dream, she saw the baby in her head. It was her baby that was meant for her; it had come into this world for her to nurture; it was her baby but it hadn't come from her belly.

'Oh my god,' she said. That was it. That was the baby she was waiting for, for whom she had been standing upside down. She didn't need to stand upside down any more. All she had to do was inverse her mind.

Anjolie put one heel on the railing, stretched her leg and bent forward. She placed her chin on her knee and looked down. There were five girls playing on the grass below. Two of them had locked their palms together and were holding them up and the other three were running in circles under their arms. *Oranges and lemons, sold for a penny, all the schoolgirls are so many. The grass is green and the rose is red, remember me till you're dead, dead, dead.* When they said 'dead' the third time, they swung their arms down and caught the girl who was under their arms. That's just like life, Anjolie thought, you run and you run, waiting to be caught in a little hug.

It had rained in the morning and the grass was wet. If I were to jump, she wondered, would I land on the grass or in the hug? The doorbell rang twice in quick succession and she ran to open the door. Dhruv stood outside with that divine smile on his face. He stepped in and she shut the door and fell into his arms. She rested her head against his shoulder. This is where I want to be, she thought, this is my spot. And then he kissed her. Her lips were like clouds and they were drifting away. She held onto his neck and kissed him. She felt his hand slide under her top and touch a breast. It feels so good, she thought, it has never felt this good before. My breasts belong to him now, they are his. And as he played with her breast, her body screamed out; she could feel every inch of it for the first time.

Dhruv moved closer to her. His face was an inch away from hers now and all she could see were his eyes. She wondered what he was thinking. But Dhruv was in a sort of dream state between waking and sleeping when one thought flows into another with no control over any of it. It was like driving a car down a slope without brakes: you just have to steer and steer and wish with all your heart that you don't crash.

He pulled her towards him and kissed her again. He touched her lips with his fingers. He wanted to fit into her mouth like a trumpet, he wanted to feel the cool brass edges sink into her warm mouth and blow out music.

And then he called her Tulsi.

At first she smiled a little smile inside her mouth. He loves me so much that he calls me by the name of his wife, she whispered to herself. Then the name got louder and she pulled herself away from his arms.

'Anjolie,' she said. 'It means beautiful angel in French.'

'That's partly true,' he said. 'But whether you're an angel or the devil, I don't yet know.'

'I guess you'll find out soon enough,' she said and moved closer.

Anjolie looked at his flickering eyes and dimpled cheeks and wished he would stop loving his wife but deep down she knew he would never stop loving her, just as she would never stop loving Neel.

He was *her* Dhruv now, when she was in his arms, he in hers. But as the afternoon wore into evening and he stood up and walked towards the door, there was a shadow following him and shadows were like people – they had a name and a face and this one had short brown hair.

—

Dhruv's footsteps got louder and louder on the floor. He walked past the guest bedroom and stopped. He turned around. The twin beds were separated. His wife lay on the floor with an incomplete expression on her face, an unfinished painting on the easel that made him want to cry. There were paints piled up on the bedside table and there was blood on the floor and on her hand. He almost screamed.

Tulsi opened her eyes and saw Dhruv looking at her woefully. And then it all came back to her. She had set up her canvas in the middle of the guest bedroom and the canvas had stood erect, waiting for her. She had been scared to touch it at first – what if she disappointed the canvas with her strokes?

That's when she pulled out a cigarette and held it upside down, gently rolling it back and forth between her fingers. When the tobacco fell out, she took out the little polythene bag from Dhruv's jeans and powdered the weed in the palm of her hand, tossing out the stems and seeds. She packed it tightly into the empty cigarette and twisted the end before lighting it. She inhaled deeply and let the smoke warm her lungs. When she finally exhaled, she was on a merry-go-round and she was seeing the same paints over and over again, she was thinking the same thoughts over and over again – it was all happening so fast and yet incredibly slow – and when she finished the joint, she realized she was thinking too many thoughts all at once and she panicked. She picked up the phone to tell Dhruv she was having a panic attack but his phone rang and rang. She had a sinking feeling that something terrible was about to happen.

The mind is its own place and in itself can make a heaven of hell and a hell of heaven. That's what Milton's Satan said to himself after his fall from heaven, she thought and then she remembered something Dhruv had told her long ago: that you made the trip what you wanted it to be. You could control it or it could control you. Either way it was all up to you.

She captured the moment as it was fleeing away and

she turned it around. She got out of her panic attack and she opened a bottle of paint. She painted while the leaves changed colour – first they became radiant and then they began to fade – and as evening fell, she fell to the floor with a bottle of paint. She had done her deed for the day. She had changed the plain white canvas into a painting and now the world looked a little bit different, for her painting had added itself to the picture of the world.

She closed her eyes and felt her heart pounding. She heard footsteps getting louder and louder on the floor. She opened her eyes and saw that the footsteps belonged to Dhruv. What she didn't see was that the bottle of paint that had fallen with her was a bottle of blood-red paint.

Dhruv saw the bottle and sank to the floor in relief. He lay next to her, his cheek touching hers, and his thigh brushed against hers aimlessly. I wonder if he can hear footsteps too, Tulsi thought. I wonder if he can hear the footsteps of our little girl.

But all he could hear was the beating of his heart when he kissed Anjolie and he was thinking that it had been years since he had kissed Tulsi like that in the mouth. So he rolled over to kiss her, just to see what it would feel like now. He leaned over her and put his lips against hers and when he was about to find out, Tulsi moved her face away.

'I have a lot on my mind,' she said.

And so they lay on the floor, each one looking at the motionless fan, thinking their own thoughts, one head away from the other, Dhruv thinking of Anjolie's lips and Tulsi thinking of her canvas, and they wouldn't kiss and make love to each other again for many, many months to come.

Five for silver,
Six for gold

8

The apartment was full of smoke. A fire burned in the middle of the living room. A baby girl sat in a green pattu pavadai in her father's lap while he poured ghee into the flames at rhythmic intervals. His forehead was marked with ash, his poonal hung over the folds on his belly and the little girl clung to it from time to time.

It was her first birthday. Later in the evening, they would pierce a hole through each ear so that she could wear her mother's diamonds and rubies and emeralds. A four-year-old boy sat near his father gazing at the flames. He didn't look a day older than three. He didn't seem to have grown at all since the last time he sat looking at flames. That was when his mother was burning instead of twigs.

Leela died a year ago. Three-sixty-five days in the life of a one-year-old is a lifetime. It's a couple of months for a giant tortoise and several lifetimes for a fruit fly. A year ago, on the same day, I had just performed Pooja's abortion when Leela went into labour. When I was delivering her baby, Leela's breathing became laboured and she began to cough uncontrollably. Her blood pressure dropped and she had a cardiac arrest. I called in the team and we began to give her CPR. Outside the room, in the silent corridor, I knew they could hear her cry, the beautiful baby who would never be in her mother's arms. When I walked out, they were distributing laddoos with smiles on their faces and when they saw me, they wanted to know if it was a boy or a girl. A girl, I said, and they froze. They knew from the look on my face that something terrible had happened. Was the baby all right? Did she have ten fingers and ten toes? The baby is perfectly fine, I said. Leela isn't. We are trying everything to revive her. I went back inside. But Leela disappeared into another world, leaving behind a pale body that reminded me of my first cadaver in medical college. The nurse took the baby in her arms and looked at me for a sign. Should she bathe her? Yes, of course, I nodded. I went out and told them that we had lost Leela. Her mother, father and husband stared at me in disbelief as I tried to explain what had happened. She may have had an amniotic fluid embolism, I said. It's a rare obstetric emergency in which amniotic fluid suddenly enters the mother's bloodstream and causes cardio-respiratory collapse.

We walked into the room and her three-year-old son saw his mother and screamed. His father picked him up. I told them that the only way we could determine the true cause of her death was to perform an autopsy. But orthodox Hindus would never cut open a dead body. When a person departs from this world, his survivors consecrate his death for his future happiness in the next world because for a Hindu the value of the next world is higher than the present one. The sutras say, 'Through the samskaras after birth, one conquers this earth; through the samskaras after death, the heaven.'

If that's what you say, we believe you. A post-mortem is not required, her father's meek voice entered my ears. Her mother began to cry and he hugged her. Her husband clutched his son in anguish. They stood in the room like that, Mr and Mrs Srinivasan in each other's arms and the young Mr Srinivasan holding his wailing son. I walked out of the room looking at the vitrified tiles that led me to my private bathroom. I wanted to vomit. I splashed cold water on my face and shut myself in the consultation room. I had lost patients before but to lose a mother at childbirth is unbearable. I wished her family would harass me and yell at me, but they stood motionless and unquestioning. They believed I could do no wrong. They accepted whatever I told them and that was what killed me.

I thought about Leela's cherubic face. Even in the delivery room in her hospital gown, she had a small black dot on her forehead. She had died a sumangali, auspiciously. Only, she had died too young. She was twenty-four.

I felt anger well up inside me. I wanted to go to her mother-in-law and scream: Are you happy now? Your daughter-in-law has died unwidowed just like you wanted. Medically, there was nothing I could have done to save her. An amniotic fluid embolism is a rare and not fully understood medical emergency. You can't diagnose it, you can't treat it. But I was angry with myself for the twinge of jealousy I had felt every time Leela walked into my consultation room with a coy smile on her face, looking pristine and untarnished, as if life had always been kind to her and she to it, as if they had made a pact to smoothly ride the journey together without making mistakes. And that, I realized, was the saddest part; that she had never experimented, never explored, never fallen down to fit the pieces of herself back together, that she had sailed slickly along, making everyone happy.

Her death coincided with her daughter's birth and they would always be like parallel train tracks that never meet. It was as if her heart had waited, waited patiently for twenty-four years to give birth to that baby before collapsing. I sat looking at the boy who sat looking at the flames that sat looking at the little girl who, for one moment, looked at me. Her eyes glowed in the light of the flames and she seemed to be asking me why, why I had not saved her mother and why I had brought her into this world motherless and naked like an ill-fated twig.

The colourful cuckoo pushed the door open, moved its tiny beak and crowed three times. Pooja lay in bed and played with an empty chocolate box, listening to 'Riders on the Storm'. Her mother walked in then with a big smile. 'It's here!' she said and placed an envelope on the bed.

It was addressed to Ms Pooja Khanna. From the Department of Film, Television and Digital Media, University of California, Los Angeles.

'Don't you want to open it, sweetie?'

She picked up the envelope, tore it open and pulled out an icy sheet of paper that smelt like America. Her aunt had once sent her a pair of Levi's jeans from there and it had smelt just like that till she wore it. Then it smelt like a pair of jeans.

Dear Ms Khanna,

We are happy to offer you admission to the University of California, Los Angeles and are delighted to welcome you as a member of the class of 2003...

She had finally woken up. The nightmare had ended. She would step into a new country with new faces and new trees and Sunil would disappear inside her head like a mothball inside a closet. She put down the letter. Sunlight flooded in through the window and soaked every word with its brightness, its lightness, illuminating the world around her. She thought of the woman she saw that morning when the sun disappeared behind the sky and of her little boy who would always remain a little boy in all his memories with his mother.

She had walked barefoot into the operation theatre. The floor was cold and her feet tingled with every step. A nurse shaved her pubic hair with a man's razor and dressed her in a blue hospital gown that exposed her bottom. This will be over soon, this will be over soon, she repeated to herself like a sacred mantra, and then the blood will begin to flow.

The anaesthetist entered the room: a papier maché masked face followed by a green short-sleeved shirt and green drawstring pants. Matching green socks took long steps. She felt a sudden stab in her vein; liquid flowed into her stream of consciousness and the room dissolved into mist.

When she finally woke up, she was lying alone in a white recovering room, the anaesthesia fading away and the blood leaking out – and she touched her pubis. It was smooth like a soft shaved head. That's when she heard the cries; first the baby's and then the others'. But what made her twist and turn on her rubber sheet was the echo of the little boy's shriek. She rang for the nurse and a wobbly old lady popped into the room and told her that a woman had died in the opposite room while giving birth; a woman with a three-year-old son.

Then it all came back to her. She remembered looking at the woman a few hours earlier, while they sat in the waiting room, waiting to go to their allotted rooms for their allotted procedures: a tormented sixteen-year-old who would end her pregnancy and a contented twenty-four-year-old who would give birth.

For contented was the word that came to mind when Pooja saw the woman walk in in a black and white maternity dress followed by her parents, her husband and her toddler in a stately line. Contented was the word that came to mind when the woman sat next to her with deep pink lipstick over a satisfied smile, a minuscule dot on her forehead and impeccably combed straight hair while Pooja fiddled with her disobedient curls and tried to pick herself up one more time. And for a moment, just for a moment, Pooja wished she was her, sitting next to her dear mother with a baby inside her stomach. Instead, she squeezed her belly and shuffled in her seat.

And then she spotted Anu. Her dear friend entered the clinic like a burst of carnations in a yellow sundress. She was carrying a picnic basket with sandwiches, beach towels and sunscreen lotion. They had lied to their mothers about spending the day at the beach with their classmates – somewhere on the way to Mahabalipuram, they had said. When they went back to Pooja's house from the hospital without a tan, Anu promptly told her mother, 'Aunty, sunscreen lotion really works!'

—

'I'm so proud of you!' her mother said now, leaning forward to kiss her cheek, her eyes filling with tears, tears of joy and of anticipation.

But Pooja was looking at the bougainvillea in the garden. They looked like vaudeville merkins in the afternoon sun and she could smell the Lakme sunscreen lotion that she had spread all over her body that day.

Her mother went to the kitchen to make gulab jamuns. She always made gulab jamuns when there was good news. It was her way of giving back to the world the sweetness that it had given her. That dark blue evening when Pooja came back from the hospital, all she told her mother was, 'Make gulab jamuns, mama.' And her mother was delighted, even though her daughter looked like a wounded puppy, because this was the first time her Pooja had spoken of food in months. 'My baby is back!' was all she said and went straight to the kitchen.

Pooja looked in the mirror. She would lose five kilos before going to America, she said to herself. She stood sideways and sucked in her stomach. Six kilos, she decided, and I have three months' time. I'll start tomorrow after having gulab jamuns today.

Her mother called her to the dining room. There were fresh gulab jamuns on the table. Pooja and her mother served themselves. When her father came home, they would surprise him with the letter, they decided.

'I have only partial scholarship, mama,' Pooja said. 'Can papa pay for the rest?'

'Of course he can, darling. We have so many shares that are just sitting in cupboards. And then there's the flat in Kotturpuram.'

'We need to go shopping.'

'Yes. We need to buy new clothes and a new suitcase to carry them in!'

'I'm going to California. I won't need winter clothes.'

'We'll call Sonia mausi and ask her what you'll need.'

'I'll need jackets.'

'You'll need a new pair of jeans.'

When the word jeans entered her head, she remembered that she needed to go on a diet first. She needed to lose six kilos before slipping into new Levi's. Pooja put the jamun in her mouth and licked her fingers clean.

'This is my last gulab jamun,' she said and went back to her room.

Her mother sat by herself and tears spilled from her eyes; they dripped over her cheeks, over her soft pink lips and into her mouth.

They tasted like the sea.

9

Midnight under the Madras sky. A cloud that looks like a giant tortoise is leisurely gliding towards another giant – a bear, perhaps, or a unicorn, its horns spreading across the great expanse, turning indigo into smoky white. There are no stars. They are hidden behind the tortoise and unicorn, shimmering unseen. The horns move away by themselves, past the tortoise, past the unicorn that has now become a horse like any other. I think of Laura's glass menagerie. My cloud animals are more fragile and when I wake up in the morning they will be gone.

I look at Sid sprawled across my bed. In the morning he will be gone too. He is taking a break from the travelogue and going on a new assignment to New York for the *Lonely Planet*. I need the money, he says. Plus, it's instant gratification. This travelogue of mine, he says, I don't know if it'll ever see the light of day.

Pooja came to say goodbye today. She would be studying film in the same place Jim Morrison did, she said breathlessly. She had healed, she said. She had stopped her medication and life couldn't be better. But you need to eat more, I said, looking at her lollipop frame, and I made her promise to undergo counselling for eating disorder.

Tulsi hadn't come to me for several months. When she finally did, she was a different woman. Her hair had grown longer and her big brown eyes had new depth. There was an ocean trapped between them.

'Sorry I disappeared on you like that,' she said.

'If my patients don't need me, it's a good thing,' I said. 'They usually come to me when something is wrong.'

'Or when something is terribly right,' she said and smiled. 'I want to adopt a baby.'

She had been painting. She gave me an invitation to her *vernissage* at the Apparao Galleries. I went for it and caught a glimpse of her world. The mezzanine terrace was packed with a loud advertising gang and quiet artists in unbranded clothes. Both cliques were drinking themselves silly. Her paintings were spectacular. They reminded me of what Aldous Huxley said in his recollection of a mescaline trip. What the rest of us see only under the influence of mescaline, the artist is congenitally equipped to see all the time.

The opening was a hit. *The Hindu* said her work was passionate and overwhelmingly diverse. *The Times of India* said her lines melted into the canvas and her colours resonated with emotion.

I felt wonderful that evening at the Apparao Galleries. Tulsi looked resplendent beside her canvasses. She had put her infertility behind her and forged ahead with a new chapter in her life. At that moment I felt my job was done. I am not a fertility enthusiast. When methods of assisted reproductive technology fail, I bring up adoption, not IVF. There are so many unwanted baby girls in this country. Wouldn't it be delightful to take one of them home instead of trying to turn the world around to conceive? Besides, IVF costs a fortune. Even for women under thirty-five, the success rate is a mere 30 per cent. How can I gamble away a couple's hard-earned money as if it were a game of poker? When they come to me for the procedure, I counsel adoption instead. But Tulsi had arrived at the decision on her own and I was looking at her like a proud parent. Ironically, it is at moments like these – that have nothing whatsoever to do with medicine – that I feel like a true gynaecologist.

If you look up the meaning of gynaecology, you will find that it is derived from the Greek *gynaikos* meaning woman and *logia* meaning study. Gynaecology is the study of women and a gynaecologist is a student of women. I am a student of women, I tell myself, and each day I learn something new. I have learnt that if Megha wanted to abort her foetus she must have been suffering deeply. Why else would a woman want to abort her baby because it's a girl? I don't condemn abortion, far from it. In fact, one of the reasons why I chose this profession was to do abortions on women without making them feel like scoundrels. But sex-selective abortion is a different ballgame. Occasionally a woman would come to me for it and I would turn her away curtly. But when I saw Megha's waiflike frame enter the room with the demon duck of doom, I became less opinionated and more understanding. I will not perform such an abortion but at least I can turn them down with grace.

The sky has turned deep blue. Stars are sprinkled across it like grains of sugar and form a grid pattern of dots against the darkness. I draw lines from dot to dot as if it is a giant kolam that will bestow prosperity to the world, and distinguish a wolf, a lizard, a lion and a little horse.

———

It was an expressionless sky. The kind of sky Zubeida had seen when she went to the photo studio to take a picture of the family. While the photographer arranged the members like fruits in a basket – the bearded husband to the right, his plump wife to the left holding a baby in her arms, a little boy to her left and a little boy to her right and one little boy between them – if she had looked the other way instead of at the camera, if she had looked at the painted sky behind her, it would have looked exactly like that.

Her breasts were huge. Her baby suckled on one and then fell asleep. Now I can eat biryani, she thought, buttoning her blouse and opening the fridge, her mouth watering at the thought of heating up yesterday's biryani and biting into sizzling pieces of mutton. She was hungry all the time because she was still breastfeeding the last one, she said to herself, but deep down she knew that she would be hungry even if she wasn't, because she loved to eat.

While her clothes got tighter with every baby, her husband remained thin. He ate twice as much as her and then asked for another helping. She wondered where all that food went. He didn't lift a finger except to collect rupee notes behind his rosewood desk at the lehenga shop. And when he wasn't counting notes, he was sitting on a mat facing the Qibla and praying. So where did all that energy go? Perhaps, she thought, in some bizarre spiritual equation between man and god, the energy was consumed in prayer.

Maybe I should pray too, Zubeida thought, looking at the folds around her belly. Maybe it would melt away the fat. And maybe, just maybe, there was a god somewhere from here to Mecca, going by one of his ninety-nine names.

She pulled out a dusty prayer mat and rolled it out on the floor. She closed her eyes. She brought her hands to her shoulders and then folded them on her chest. She bowed and put her hands on her knees. She could smell the biryani that was now piping hot on the stove. It tickled her nose and made her mouth water. She rolled up the mat and went to the kitchen. I'll eat now and pray later, she decided.

The biryani melted in her mouth and within seconds her plate was empty. She heaped more on her plate and then some more and soon it was all gone and she was alone again. But not for long, she said to herself. Not for long. In a few minutes, she would be in Seema's flat watching her first foreign film. And on Sunday, she was going to see Spiderman. I want to take the boys to see *Spiderman* on Sunday, she had told her husband the night before. But really it was she who wanted to see *Spiderman*. When she was a little girl, she saw *Superman* at her uncle's house in Bombay one summer. Her uncle had come back from Germany with a colour TV and VCR and she watched *Superman* with half the neighbourhood huddled together in a windowless room. She still remembered the film. It was blue. The sky was blue. Superman was blue. He turned the world backwards and turned back time and brought his girl back to life. Had she been older when she was born – older and muscular, like Superman – she would have turned the world backwards and brought her mother back to life. But such is life.

She rinsed her plate and the last traces of biryani disappeared into the sink. Her son cried in his sleep and she went to the bedroom and picked him up. You are never old enough when you are born, she thought, and you are never old enough when you die. Carrying him in her arms, she locked the door to her apartment and tiptoed across the narrow corridor to Seema's door.

Seema was newly married to Zubeida's neighbour, who had a pocket-sized shop in Burma Bazaar where he sold imported perfumes, cell-phones, iPods, DVD players and DVDs. She was a fragile-looking woman with round cheeks and when she smiled, you couldn't see her eyes.

A few weeks after the new bride had come home looking pretty and pink in her green salwar-kameez with gold sequins, Zubeida had gone over to offer her kheer and when they sat down to talk in the dingy living room, she spotted a large cardboard box lying in a corner.

'What's inside that box?' she asked Seema, trying to hide her curiosity.

'I don't know. My husband has told me never to open that box.'

'All right then, may I?'

Seema giggled nervously. She had been curious too but she had never dared to go near that box. What if there was something hideous inside? But if Zubeida wanted to open it, she wasn't going to stop her.

'Sure,' Seema said.

The two women leaned over the large cardboard box, and Zubeida opened a flap and peeped in. Inside the box were DVDs of films from all over the world. She pulled one out and grinned at Seema. It was a DVD of a Polish film.

Zubeida quickly read the stories on the backs and Seema looked at the pictures on the covers wistfully. On her third visit to Seema's flat, Zubeida convinced her that they should watch the films. Seema was scared at first.

'What if my husband finds out?'

'But your husband is in the shop from ten in the morning
to ten at night and I have never seen him come back before
eleven in the seven years that I have lived in this building.
We could watch the film in the afternoon and then wrap it
up and put it back in the box. Nobody would ever know.'

How exciting it would be to see a foreign film, Seema
thought. She would never visit these places in her lifetime.
She took out a DVD. It had a picture of a woman running
in an oversized sweater and a man's hat. Two men ran
behind her. The one with a moustache was holding onto
his hat and running behind the one without the moustache
and they were all laughing. The woman looked so happy.
Then Seema noticed that the woman who was running had
a moustache drawn on her face.

'We'll watch this one,' she said.

'It's French,' Zubeida said and pulled *Jules et Jim* out of
its case.

'Tonight I will find out how to play it.'

And so the next day Zubeida stood outside Seema's door
with her baby fast asleep in her arms. She had two whole
hours before her boys came home from school. Seema
opened the door with a naughty smile. She had already
switched on the player and put the DVD inside. Everything
was ready, she said; she just had to press play.

'Press play!' said Zubeida and plopped down.

Seema pressed the play button and sat next to Zubeida
on the floor, leaning against the old Rexene sofa with cotton
popping out of the holes. The floor was cold. The screen
was black. They heard a woman's voice. She's talking in
French, Zubeida whispered feverishly. They read the white
subtitles on the black screen, Zubeida in seconds and Seema
following after her.

You said: I love you. I said: Wait. I was going to say, take me.
You said: Go away.

And then the screen lit up.

Jules and Jim become the best of friends and fall in love with the capricious Catherine. But it is Jules who asks her to marry him. World War I breaks out and the friends are separated. At the end of the war, Catherine marries Jules and has his baby. Jim goes to to visit them and Catherine kisses Jim on the stairs. 'One is never completely in love for more than a moment,' she says and falls in love with Jim.

Seema was shocked at first but soon she became curious about this strange world so far away from hers and Zubeida sat clutching a scrawny yellow cushion and repeating Catherine's words in her head. One is never completely in love for more than a moment. Would she ever have her moment, Zubeida wondered, even once?

She looked at the television screen long after the movie had ended; she was looking beyond the screen at the wall behind it with dirty brown stains, beyond the bedroom and the covers on the bed with big blue elephants, beyond the window, beyond the mosque that you could see from the window and far beyond its little minarets that were calling and calling, calling and calling her to prayer.

—

Megha was sitting in a corner reciting the Namokar mantra when a giant bird spread its wings over her face and the whole room disappeared under its shadow.

'Khana kaun banayega?' Who's going to make lunch, her mother-in-law asked.

Was it a multiple-choice question, Megha wondered. Could she answer: Why don't you do it? Could she say that one of the three maids who sat idly in the backyard would do it? Or perhaps she could say that it was Sunita's turn to cook today. But then she remembered that Sunita had given them two grandsons and all Megha could provide were three pathetic little girls. And lunch.

So she got up and walked to the kitchen. Her mother-in-law followed, reciting the menu behind her left ear. Gatta curry, dhaniyamangodi, palak paneer, besan ki puri…

She thrust fresh spinach leaves into Megha's hands.

'The palak paneer is for the children, so you can put onions in it. Make that first.'

Megha wanted to say something, anything. She thought of an appropriate thing to say. Maybe she could ask where Sunita was. Maybe Sunita could help her with the gatta.

'Where is Sunita?' she finally asked.

Her mother-in-law frowned.

'Where is the gatta?' she corrected herself hastily.

Her mother-in-law knitted her brows and wobbled out of the kitchen. Megha began to peel the onions and ground them, her tears mingling with the tears that the onion brought to her eyes. The onions were a beautiful shade of lilac. She had been cooking onions for over a year now, ever since the orthodox Jain household decided to slacken the rules, and she had never noticed their colour. As she poured the onion paste into the heated pan, she tried to think of things in real life in the same colour. She could think of nothing. Not a single thing; not a bird or flower, not a stone or river, not even the sky when the sun coloured it at dusk in shades of violet and plum. Nothing she had ever seen was this delightful shade of lilac. That means I haven't seen enough of this world, she thought.

She stirred. It seemed as if the lilac would never change.

She wanted it to change even though it was beautiful, even though it blew her mind away, because all things must change. For if it remained the same forever it wouldn't be beautiful any more.

She looked through the kitchen window and saw her daughters playing. They raced each other to the gate and back. They never seemed to tire of the same game. She looked at the frying pan. At that instant the colour changed from lilac to a pale pinkish-brown. She liked the new colour. It was mellow and it calmed her mind.

And then she remembered the tomato puree. Usually, on a usual day, under a usual sky, she would have been waiting impatiently for the onions to fry, she would have been waiting to pour in the tomato puree and be done with it; but today was different, even the sky looked different through the window. There was a sense of peace about the kitchen, it was cooler than yesterday and she knew the temperature had changed only in her head. She had been so fascinated watching the pan that she had forgotten to add the tomato puree. She poured it in. I know what colour this is, she said to herself. It was tomato red, just like the sari with golden mangoes that she was wearing when she walked into the house for the first time.

The grandfather clock in the living room struck twelve. The clock was older than her. The same clock had been striking year after year for decades. I wonder who was in the kitchen before I was born, she thought, watching the frying pan as the clock struck twelve. Under the same sun thirty years ago, by the same window watching other children play, she saw her mother-in-law looking pale and gauzy like filter paper, waiting for the tomatoes to fry.

—

I met Shanti at a doctors' conference. She looked years older than the last time I saw her. I wondered how much I had aged. But we had both aged, mentally, physically and chronologically, in the last fifteen years since we left medical school.

She had married a radiologist, given birth to three children and no doubt delivered several. I was unmarried at the age of thirty-nine. Shanti, I thought with a twinge of jealousy, had definitely done something right.

When we were in med school together, we shared the same room, the same friends, the same teachers and once, even the same man. We were on the same shift during our internship when we did hospital duties. We assisted many births and deaths at the General Hospital in Royapettah and when we couldn't keep our eyes open after being on shift for twenty-four hours at a stretch, we would sneak into my car and share a cigarette. Then we would come back and attend to terminally ill patients with renewed enthusiasm.

I could read Shanti's thoughts and she mine. I could tell how long she would take to walk to my car in her childish steps while I waited for her in the parking lot. We would giggle like schoolgirls when we left the hospital, our clothes smelling of pain and poverty and Dettol and death. And deliveries, 'bledy deliveries!' as Shanti would say.

Shanti loved jewellery. She would match them to her sari while I dragged myself to hospital in a mix-and-match salwar-kameez. Shanti's father owned a tea shop on Mount Road and her mother worked at Apollo Hospital. Her mother cleaned the hospital floors with hundreds of other maids. Her mother worked two shifts a day to see

her through school. Unlike her four brothers and most of
the neighbourhood children, Shanti loved to study. She
won a scholarship to study medicine. She was a scholarship
student, unlike the rest of us, and her English wasn't good
because she had been schooled in a corporation school that
smelt like the hospital we trained in.

But it was only on the last day of our internship that I
found out how she bought all that jewellery. She took money
from pregnant women and told them the sex of their unborn
child.

I ran out of the hospital when I found out and didn't take
any of her calls. When she came home, I told my mother to
tell her that I was away. But I knew she knew I was there. I
was filled with disgust and I ran and ran from her till she left
Madras and never came back. Now, fifteen years later, I saw
her through the crowded conference room and her childish
steps gave her away at once.

She recognized me the same instant and smiled. She
looked fifteen years older but her smile hadn't aged a day.
She walked up to me. It was obvious that she had forgiven
me for running away, but had I forgiven her?

When she spoke to me she was a different person. Her
English had improved over the years and there was no trace
of a south Indian accent in her voice. In its place was a north
Indian accent that sprang up every time she said guy-ne-co-
low-g and instead of artificial gemstones, elegant diamonds
nestled against her newly wrinkled throat.

She lived in Kurukshetra, she said.

Kurukshetra, I said to myself, that certainly rang a bell.
Kurukshetra was in Haryana, the state with the lowest
female sex ratio. According to the 2001 census, the sex

ratio in Haryana had declined even further, from 869 to 820 females per 1000 males. The lowest ratio in the state was in Kurukshetra where there were barely 770 females per 1000 males. Sex-selective abortions were abundant and sex determination was the norm.

'So do you have daughters or sons?' I asked.

'I have three beautiful girls,' she said. 'And you?'

I was going to tell her about Sid, and then I changed my mind. 'I'm still single,' I said and for a moment I saw a look of concern flash through her eyes. 'And ready to mingle,' I added.

It was a three-day conference. We caught up with each other on coffee breaks. She showed me pictures of her daughters. They were beautiful.

'So how did you meet Mr Right?' I asked.

'For all the wrong reasons,' she said and something flashed through her eyes. But it had been a long time since I read those eyes and I had forgotten how to read them.

'Mummy doesn't work at Apollo any more,' she said. 'She lives with me. Daddy died a few years back. He drank himself to death and my brothers are on the way.'

'How is practice?' we both uttered at the same time.

'We have a fertility clinic,' she said and stirred her tea without looking at me. And that's when I read it, I read what she was hiding in her eyes.

I had heard about doctor couples who had 'fertility clinics' on the highways of Punjab and Haryana, where sex-selective abortions were performed. I had heard about a racket that involved radiologists, owners of ultrasound machines and gynaecologists. Despite warnings against aborting the first child, 10 to 20 per cent did. About 80 per cent aborted the second and 95 per cent the third. According to an estimate, there were over 80 per cent non-institutional deliveries in Haryana alone. Exploiting the opportunity to the hilt, quacks even professed to disclose the sex of the foetus at ten weeks. In this industry, there were eager consumers and equally eager service providers.

Shanti looked at me. She knew I knew.

'At least in Haryana we abort the foetus,' she said. 'In other states, the unwanted newborn is killed.'

This was not far from the truth. I had read that a professional killer often performs the ritual by swaddling the newborn in a wet cloth or giving her a spoonful of paddy grain with milk. Sometimes the mother hires a sweeper to poison the baby for twenty-five rupees.

In February 2007, the police would find 390 body parts from foetuses and newborn babies buried in the backyard of a Christian missionary hospital in Ratlam, Madhya Pradesh. The government would set up special homes to adopt unwanted girls. 'What we are saying to people is have your children, don't kill them. And if you don't want a girl child, leave her to us.' They would try to clamp down on doctors violating the law that bans prenatal sex determination tests, and a national campaign with the slogan 'My Strength, My Daughter' would be launched, but it would make no difference. For the advertising slogan of diagnostic teams with ultrasound machines that predict the sex of the unborn child is catchier. *Only 600 rupees now: save 50,000 rupees later!*

'I don't expect you to understand,' Shanti said. 'You were born with a silver spoon.'

She came into the world with nothing, like three hundred million others in India. How would I know the lives of all these people? How would I know the pain? The closest I had come to it was Megha, and her family was rolling in wealth. What about the rest?

I left Shanti sitting at the table, but this time I said goodbye.

10

Tulsi slid into a black cocktail dress and dabbed some red lipstick on. She thought of the jazz concert that they were going to at the Taj. Dhruv was waiting for her in the car. He needed to make a phone call, so he had gone ahead to the car park. She reread the invitation. There would be cocktails. She could certainly use a drink tonight.

She ran down the stairs in black stilettos with black roses on the toes and got into the car. She turned on the radio. 'This is Chennai's only English radio station, Chennai Live 104.8 FM, and this is Sano here, bringing to you Live Talk. We have our own Kollywood superhero with us today, the one and only Quick Gun Murugan!'

Tulsi turned up the volume. The outlandish Quick Gun Murugan came on air and spoke about how much he liked masala dosas. Then he described his latest film where he kicks his mortal enemy Rice Plate Reddy's ass.

'You will thrill to see a killing four people with one bullet. You will thrill to see a typical cowboy,' he said boorishly.

Dhruv did an imitation. 'These cheaters are making vegetarians to nan-vegetarians hotel. Rascals! I will teach them how to behave.'

Tulsi laughed and looked at Dhruv, love gushing from her eyes. He always brought a smile to her face, even after all these years.

'I will teach *you* how to behave,' she said and took his left hand and placed it on her thigh.

It lay there limply for a moment and then Dhruv had to slow down at Gemini Circle so he took his hand back and changed gears. Cars honked around them in a cacophony as the white Accent inched its way through the mayhem.

'Switch it back to the CD player, sweetie. I was listening to "Comfortably Dumb",' said Dhruv.

'That, my darling, is a Floydian slip!' said Tulsi and felt very proud of herself. For it was usually Dhruv who said things like that.

Dhruv smiled in acknowledgement of her wit. The lights turned green and the car glided under the Gemini Flyover and touched Nungambakkam High Road.

They were at the Taj. The giant chandelier bathed the air with crystalline light and everybody was glowing, like jewels in a shop window. Dhruv was already at the other end of the ballroom talking to someone and Tulsi walked to the bar and got herself a whisky on the rocks. She took a voluminous swig and looked around. The concert was about to begin and they were closing the bar. A woman entered the room and all the men turned their heads like sunflowers in a field. She was wearing a red sundress and her long hair fell over her shoulders on either side. There should be a law against being this beautiful, Tulsi thought but other than the law of gravity, she couldn't think of anything.

The woman was looking in one direction. She was looking at someone through the crowded room, who turned his head – like the last sunflower in the field – and looked at her. He was wearing a grey shirt over a pair of jeans that Tulsi knew so well that she didn't have to see his face to know who it was.

Dhruv was shocked to see the woman. When Dhruv was shocked, he looked pokerfaced and nobody would know that he was shocked. But Tulsi knew that look – that was how he had looked at her the night of his farewell party when he said goodbye to everyone and hello to her. He was singing a *Doors* song and a hundred expressions fleeted across his eyes like windows in a moving train but in that one instant when he saw her enter the room, he had that look, that look of recognizing without recognition, that look of knowing without knowledge, that look of seeing without being seen.

Tulsi got another drink and looked around the room. She was surrounded by strangers of all shapes, sizes and colours. This looks like a zoo, she thought, that specializes in one species: the human being. She could never fathom the word 'being' as a noun, it was always a past participle in her head. If she had looked up the definition of the word 'being', it would have said: the fact of existing; existence as opposed to non-existence. It was no wonder that she couldn't envisage the word as a noun, for that was exactly what Tulsi had been fighting all her life. She had been fighting existence. And now she did not want to merely exist, she wanted to rise above existence like a mushroom cloud over the world. She wanted to live.

Since the day she started painting, she had felt life throbbing inside her. Even Dhruv had recognized that. He had come back home and lain next to her on the floor and told her it was magnificent, that she was magnificent that day. It was the first time she was painting without trying to make a painting of it, he said. She told him he was right, she had finally realized it was the verb that mattered and not the noun. She had felt a tremendous desire to pull out her Oxford Dictionary just then and check the definition of 'verb'. And if she had, it would have said: any of a class of words expressing an action performed or state suffered or experienced by a subject. She was the subject and her life was the state she would finally experience. And Dhruv understood, he understood by that one sentence her entire life and he brought his lips close to hers but she uttered something about having a lot on her mind and turned her head away.

Dhruv walked towards the woman in the red sundress and then led her to Tulsi with a hand around her waist. She introduced herself as Anjolie Cartier. She had a French name, she had French lips but her eyes were Indian. Dhruv stood next to her and introduced Tulsi as his wife. Tulsi, she added insignificantly, looking up at Anjolie who was three-and-a-half inches taller than her in *her* stilettos. There was something about the way he was looking at her, but then the ballroom went dark and the band began to play.

———

The soprano's velvet voice filled the living room, resonating with hope and devotion as the orchestra played with remarkable finesse. Three years have elapsed since Pinkerton left Butterfly with the promise to return to her. Suzuki, convinced that Pinkerton has deserted her mistress, is kneeling in front of a Buddha and praying. Butterfly is hopeful. Chiding her maid for not believing in him, she paints a picture of his homecoming.

Anjolie lay on the sofa with her eyes closed, listening to Puccini as Dhruv climbed the staircase, entered her corridor and rang the doorbell twice in quick succession. She knew it was him from the ringing, that double ring which thrilled her ears and sang into them, wiping the soprano's voice into oblivion. She opened the door and shut it as soon as he entered the flat. They fell into each other's arms and kissed. They moved towards the sofa kissing and he fell back and pulled her towards him. She sat on him, her head leaning against his shoulder, her thighs spread with one leg on either side of him, bent at the knees. She could have crushed him between her thighs and eaten him in one big gulp so he would stay inside her forever, but she leaned back and looked at his face. He had splashed water on it and it had dried up but his lashes were still wet and curled at the ends like lilies. She could see the bookshelf through his lashes, she could see the books, they looked like matchsticks and the whole world looked tiny.

The world has really shrunk, she thought. It had dwindled to the size of a pea at the jazz concert three months ago when Dhruv had expanded and filled the ballroom; she couldn't see the saxophonist, she couldn't hear the drums – all she could feel was him sitting next to his pretty little wife.

And now he had dilated again, and she tore herself away from him and walked up to the bookshelf. Behind her, he slowly constricted, becoming one size smaller with every step.

'What's the matter?' he asked.

'Everything's the matter,' she said, 'because everything doesn't matter and all that matters is you.'

'Sweetheart.'

'I can't work. I can't paint. I think I'm losing it!'

'I think about you all the time too, you know.'

'One day this will end and then our worlds will fall apart.'

'It doesn't have to end.'

'Don't you see it has to end one day? We can't go on like this forever. How long can we keep it up?'

'Why are you beating yourself up over it? This is wonderful and I love you. That's all there is to it.'

'That's the difference between you and me. You live in the moment and I don't. I can't help thinking about what will happen tomorrow. Every time I kiss you, I don't know if it's the last time.'

'Sweetheart...'

'But I've got to change that! Don't you see I've got to pull myself together and change that?'

Anjolie looked away from him and pulled out *The Bell Jar* from the bookshelf. The cover had a picture of a woman with bright yellow hair. Her lips were crimson and her face was orange. She looked as if Andy Warhol had reduced her to a silkscreen print. Anjolie heaved a sigh of relief. Finally she was looking at a book and not a pathetic little matchstick. One day this would all end, and she would have to erase him from her mind with a scent eraser like the ones she used in school when she made mistakes in her sums; the number would be rubbed away but there would always be a silent groove in the notebook reminding you of the erased figure, and if you were to put your face against it, you would smell the scent of the eraser on the page.

Dhruv looked at Anjolie. She was looking at a book and seemed miles away. Her raven-black hair covered her

profile and he could only see the tip of a nose and opaque
black eyes. She looked as mysterious as she did the first time
he saw her. He didn't love her then, he just wanted to see
her and see her, and one day he had woken up and realized
that he had fallen in love.

His phone rang.

'I'm at a friend's place. Yes, I'll be home for dinner...
Sure, omelettes sound fine...'

Anjolie closed her ears. She didn't want to hear another
word of the damned conjugal chatter but she could still
hear him even with a hand cupped over each ear, talking
to his little wife. She removed her hands from her ears,
pulled out Samuel Beckett from the bookshelf and opened
a page.

Vladimir:
I remain in the dark.
Estragon:
This is how it is.
He reflects.

Anjolie reflected. She knew a fraction of her was waiting
to be over and done with it, when one of them would be
gone and the other would be left standing alone. It was
better than the anticipation of it, but who would be gone
and who would be left standing alone?

Dhruv hung up the phone and drew near. He nibbled
at her neck and her heartache dissolved, her anguish
evaporated and she smiled at the pure joy of being in his
arms again.

'Maybe you're right,' she said. 'Why beat myself over it?
You're mine now and that's all that matters.'

'I'm yours,' he said and kissed her neck again, and

when he was finished she was left with a mark that faintly resembled a horseshoe.

I will keep it for good luck, Anjolie thought and watched him go.

Outside, there was a clear, cloudless daytime sky, the sort of sky that is characteristic of Madras in July, when summer has gone and reappeared in Europe. The summer festival was being celebrated in Barcelona and a thousand plays were being staged in Avignon where people were drinking wine at every corner, and at the Love Parade in Berlin, a million people were dancing in the streets to celebrate love and hedonism; but here in Madras, it was just July. Summer was over and school had begun, and it was hot, it was terribly hot, hotter than Europe where it was summer now.

———

While the leaves turned orange in other parts of the world, colouring the landscape in yellows, ochres and reds, in Madras it remained bright green. The sun blazed through the sky with a vengeance and the air was sticky like honey.

Dhruv walked into his sun-drenched apartment and removed his Nikes. He had been running a lot these days. He walked around the room in his skin-coloured cotton socks and poured himself a beer. He had another three dozen pairs of identical socks sitting in his closet. He always wore the same skin-coloured cotton socks. This way, he figured, he didn't have to look for a matching pair. And now his life had become like his socks. There were three of them and he didn't know which ones would make the matching pair.

He picked up his guitar and sat by the window. He strummed his fingers along the bass strings. He played a few notes high and then gradually descended, building intensity as he moved down the neck. He messed around with the notes until he got a finger-picking pattern he liked and the words of his song appeared.

She fed her cat every day
She fed him candy and cake
The cat left her and ran away
But she, but she...
But she continued to bake.

The key turned inside the lock, the doorknob creaked clockwise and the door flung wide open. Tulsi darted inside and flung her bag on the dining table.

'Guess what?' she said animatedly.

'You got second prize in a beauty contest?' Dhruv teased.

'Your commercial has been approved by the client. You're going to Paris!'

Dhruv couldn't believe his ears. He had written that commercial for fun. It was for a new brand of Indian jeans. He had smoked a large joint and imagined Anjolie doing the headstand in a pair of jeans and he had written it just for a lark and presented it to the client.

It was set in Paris with the Eiffel Tower in the background. You see a tourist sitting down and looking at the tower in amazement. The first shot is in the morning and the next one at noon and then mid-afternoon and the last shot is early evening. All through the day you see the same tourist looking at the tower. Then the camera zooms in and you realize that he's not looking at the tower but at a woman who is doing a headstand with her hands making a triangle on the ground and her legs extended towards the sky. She is wearing jeans that fit snugly around her incredibly toned butt. She has been in that pose all day and it is she that he has been looking at all along. In the end, you find out that he is admiring neither the Eiffel Tower nor the pose but her well-toned bottom and then the camera zooms in on the label and the brand name that was upside down flips over and adjusts itself right side up.

'Did you hear me?' Tulsi said.

'Yup. I can't believe it.'

'Oh, baby, you're going to have a blast! It's autumn in Paris now.'

'Hey, hey, go slow, babe. I'm not going to believe anything till I talk to the client.'

'You have a post-lunch meeting with him on Friday. Till then all you have to do is find a woman who can stand on her head.'

I've found her, he thought. I found her long ago and now I don't know what to do.

———

Anjolie sat in front of her husband at Bella Ciao, the Italian restaurant by the sea. You couldn't see the sea from here but you could feel it in your bones. She picked up her glass of red wine from the cement table and held it below her eyes. The sea breeze entered her nostrils and filled her lungs with weightless air, lifting her one millionth of a metre above her seat.

That was the best part about living in Madras, she thought, sipping her wine: the sea. She would find it claustrophobic to be in a city without a sea. Somehow the knowledge that there was a deep blue ocean on one side of the city calmed her nerves. She put the bruschetta into her mouth. It tasted of an Italian summer several years ago. The tomato and olive oil melted in her mouth and she took a sip of wine to erase the memory of Antonio that had crept into her head. Was it because she had been with so many men in the past that it had become so easy for her to be unfaithful?

'You have that look in your eyes,' said Neel.

'What look?'

'The first time I saw that look was on the Paris–Madras flight when the captain announced that we would land shortly.'

'And what look is that?'

'It's a look of softness, of warmth, of something melting in your eyes; it's the look of being in love.'

She hadn't realized that she was as transparent as the glass she was holding. But Neel was one of the few people who could read her eyes. And now Dhruv had begun to do it too.

Directly above their table, dangling over a starless sky, was the moon gaping at them wide-eyed.

'Why does the moon always look the same?' she asked, changing the subject.

'It is in synchronous rotation with the earth, that's why it shows the same face at all times.'

'That's like two people married for donkey's years.'

'I guess you could say that about the earth and the moon,' said Neel, laughing.

The lamp from the table behind him illuminated his face in parts. When he moved his head, she could see his eyelashes now and then. They were long and luminous. But they did not curl at the ends like Dhruv's. They did not look like lilies.

'The surface gravity of the moon is only a sixth that of the earth. Even though your mass would be the same on the earth and the moon, if you weigh sixty kilos on earth, you would weigh about ten on the moon.'

'You know everything, don't you?' she said, half smiling, half frowning, afraid he knew about her and Dhruv.

'Sometimes I wish I did,' he said and looked deep into her guilty black eyes.

—

Anjolie plunged into the motionless consultation room and perched herself on the teakwood chair. Her long black hair was wet and fell over her shoulders and into her lap.

'Doctor,' she said, 'I'm worried that I'm infertile. Neel and I have been trying to have a baby for several months.'

'But you've been pregnant in the past,' I said.

She had an ovulation prediction kit and they had sex before, during and after ovulation. It's so ironic, I thought, how people fall in love and make love endlessly using condoms, spermicides, diaphragms, pills and shields to prevent conception, to prevent that one-in-a-millionth sperm from entering the vagina and joining the egg, and a few years later, when the spontaneity has gone out of sex, they want to have a baby. They plan their sex life around their menstrual calendar and it is no longer an act of loving but an act of conceiving.

I believe in the act of loving. I believe that the choice to reproduce is every woman's right and I try to provide them with that choice when they come to me. But there is only so much I can do in their lives. In mine, I made my choice. I didn't want to have babies, delivering them was enough for me. And in my relationship, sex is always a spontaneous act. But when the spontaneity has gone, what then?

Sid was back and we were going to spend another long weekend swimming in the sea and making love. Sometimes it was all too good to be true: the anticipation and then the exhilaration. I imagine this is how it must have been for Anjolie and Neel years ago when they were lovers, before they became man and wife battling to have a baby.

'A comprehensive infertility checkup with all the diagnostic tests can take four or five menstrual cycles,' I said. 'We can start with a pelvic examination for you and a semen analysis for your husband, if you wish.'

'I'll be back with Neel,' she said.

'For women, the tests are often invasive, painful and emotionally exhausting.'

'So what do you advise, doctor?' she asked.

I told her the same thing that I had told Tulsi years ago. Let go, let the world slip away and make love for the love of it, but she had already let the world slip away and she was making love for the love of it with Dhruv.

11

'I like Jules,' Seema said.

'I like Jim,' Zubeida said.

'But neither of us likes Catherine.'

'That's because we're jealous of her.'

'And why not? Neither of us knows what freedom is. And that is Catherine in one word. She is freedom.'

'We are free too.'

'Free to do what, Zoo? Name one thing.'

'We're free to think,' replied Zubeida and looked at the empty screen.

They had seen *Jules et Jim* seven times already and they decided not to see it again.

'What if it starts to look seen?' Seema asked, slipping the DVD into its case.

Zubeida agreed. She did not want Seema's husband to find out about their afternoon 'voyages', as they called them for want of a better code word, with the curtains drawn and the volume low as they sat in front of the television set watching foreign films.

They had seen *The Bicycle Thief, The Blue Angel, The Children of Paradise, The Eclipse, Cinema Paradiso* and *Pandora's Box*. Zubeida told Seema about the real Pandora's box. It was not a box, she explained, trying to remember the story she had read in her schooldays, but an enormous jar. It was the size of an adult human being. When Pandora opened it, it unleashed all the illnesses in the world along with fear and hunger and pain and poverty. It also unleashed hope.

Seema liked the idea of hope coming out of a box along with the miseries of the world. One hot summer night, when she was a little girl, there was a power cut and the whole family sat in the muggy living room fanning themselves and swatting mosquitoes. Seema asked her mother to call the Electricity Board to find out when the power would come back but her ninety-year-old grandmother cried out in the dark. 'Don't call them,' she wailed. 'What if they say it won't come back till tomorrow? If we don't call them, we'll never know and we can keep *hoping* it will come back any moment.'

Hope was nice, thought Seema. Hope was really, really nice, but happiness was even better.

'You know what the fortune-teller tells Antonio in *The Bicycle Thief*?' Zubeida asked.

'What?'

'You'll find the bicycle quickly or not at all.'

'Yes.'

'Sometimes I feel that way about my life. It's going to change quickly or not at all.'

'How will it change? Maybe you can have another baby, a girl this time…'

'Oh, I can't have another baby, Seem. We barely have enough money to feed the four of them. Not to mention my husband and his brothers. And me.'

'But the shop is doing well.'

'Yes, as long as there are nikkahs we'll sell our lehengas. But it's not enough to see four boys through school.'

'I know what you mean. We haven't had children yet and Yusuf is always doing the accounts. We can't buy a thing without consulting his account book. But look what he got me yesterday.'

Seema went inside and brought out a gold dress-watch inside a velvet case. It had a pearl cabochon on the crown and faceted gemstones on the face. Zubeida tried it on but it was too small for her plump wrists.

'It's beautiful, Seem. He must really love you.'

'It's from his shop. Look, it has a manufacturing defect.' Seema shook the wristwatch and a sapphire dial moved around the face.

'But you can still tell time,' said Zubeida.

Seema nodded her head earnestly as if telling time were of paramount importance. It was mostly killing time that she had been preoccupied with all these years. But now everything had changed. It had changed since the first foreign film they saw together.

Seema put the watch back in its case and went inside to put it away. Zubeida said goodbye and walked across the corridor to her flat. She left the sleeping baby on the bed and wrapped up the little hat she had made for her third son's birthday. She took out the blue satin ribbon she had preserved from a wedding gift and tied it around the gift with a little bow and then laughed as she remembered her birthdays as a little girl.

When it was your birthday on a school day you were allowed to wear a colour dress. Everybody was nice to you because they knew it was your birthday. Zubeida wanted to wear a colour dress at least twice a year. Since she didn't like celebrating her real birthday because that was the day her mother died, her grandmother let her pick a date. She chose the last week of March just before summer vacation and she zeroed in on the twenty-seventh. This way, she figured, she could wait the whole academic year to wear her colour dress. She tried to convince her grandmother to allow her a second date, one in June when school reopened *and* on twenty-seventh March, because, she reasoned, by seventh June everyone would have forgotten about twenty-seventh March. However, her grandmother had been firm about a single birthday.

But the birthday that was etched in her memory was not hers. It was Sandeep's. He had brought Eclairs for everybody and a big bar of Dairy Milk for the class teacher and he had another purple bar hidden between his schoolbooks. When the school bell rang and Zubeida started to walk home with her cousins, Sandeep ran up to her and slipped it into her hands.

'This is for you,' he said and ran away.

Zubeida placed the gift on the dining table and went to the kitchen to make pakodas for the boys for when they came home. She should call the gas company. A cylinder had gone empty that morning and she had opened the second one; she would have to call for gas first thing tomorrow. For a second, a hundred red cylinders flashed across her mind, all waiting in a basement for somebody to carry them away, each one to its own home where it would live till the end of its funereal life under a kitchen counter, tied to the stove with an umbilical cord.

———

Megha leaned over the kitchen counter and washed the potatoes in the sink. She removed the mud stuck to them and looked into the eyes as if they were babies. But they did look like babies, she thought, they looked like baby monsters from *Monsters Inc.* The kids watched the movie all the time and sometimes she felt like the little girl in monster world – only, *her* monsters were actually scary – and if she could only find a door somewhere that was hers, she would walk right through it and go back home.

She scooped out the eyes with her fingernails and peeled the skin. She sliced them and dipped them into the orange batter and fried them. Then she packed them neatly into snack boxes for the children with a generous dollop of tomato ketchup. Soon she would be off with the piping hot bhajis, taking her nephews and her eldest daughter to the Madras Boat Club where they would learn to swim in the terrace pool with a dozen other kids. Her daughter ran into the kitchen with her swimming bag and sunglasses that were too big for her tiny face.

'Mama, let's go! It's getting late!'

Megha put the Cinderella snack box and Spiderman snack boxes into a basket with three bananas and dashed out of the kitchen. The kids were already in the car. The driver took them from Purasawalkam to Boat Club Road and they counted red cars on the way and then blue ones and played word games that her daughter won thrice in a row.

She was a smart one, her little Barkha. How hard she had tried to convince her husband that she should learn swimming with the boys but he wouldn't hear of it. And then Barkha walked in and told her daddy, 'Papa, one day when we all go on a cruise and the ship sinks like the *Titanic*,

Rohit and Rahul will survive and I won't.' He threw back his head and laughed and said, 'Yes, yes, by all means learn to swim, baby!'

So now here she was, sitting by the pool, watching the kids learn to swim, and wishing she could swim in the blueness.

A woman sitting next to her smiled and asked her if that was her daughter in the little mermaid swimsuit and Megha nodded her head. 'Es. Es.'

'She's a bold one and so athletic!' she said.

'Oh, thank you,' said Megha, conscious of her English, not wanting to make mistakes. She wanted to say more, that she was bold all right but whether she was athletic she didn't know, but she didn't say a word. She wondered if she could switch to Hindi but in Chennai people didn't like it if you assumed they spoke Hindi.

She looked at the water once again and her daughter waved at her before diving in and gliding through. She was her future, this little girl in the pool who would do all the things she hadn't and stand on her own two feet and live life on her own terms. And for a moment, Megha felt as though it was she in the water, jumping and playing like the children.

———

The leafy sea dragon is perhaps the most fragile sea creature in the world. Hidden deep in the ocean's grasses, this mysterious creature resembles the seaweed that surrounds it. And you would think it was a piece of yellow-green seaweed, until it emerges suddenly, seemingly out of nowhere.

Megha walked in wearing a sea-green chiffon sari. She was alone. Her ghunghat hung loose over her head and she was smiling for the first time. Her period was three months late.

'No, no, I'm not pregnant,' she said, reading the concern on my face. 'This toh is only a late period.'

'You are severely anaemic and your body is emaciated. It's not a good idea for you to get pregnant again.'

Somehow, she seemed different this time. Even though she was still all skin and bones, a new dimension had entered her being and she looked alive. Was it because she was alone, sitting in front of me without the predatory bird looming over her? Or had something changed in her head?

She let the ghunghat slip away. Her hair was long and thick and fell in a loose plait down her back.

'Es, I know what you are telling me, doctor, but…' she began and then told me about her miserable life, switching between English, Hindi and Tamil as if they were keys in a grand piano. I was amazed at the startling fluency of this trilingual woman who had spent most of her life in silence. I didn't know what to tell her except that it was not advisable for her to get pregnant again.

I asked her to do a blood test and prescribed a contraceptive pill to start her flow. She was taking her iron tonic and vitamins regularly but it was evident that she was not getting enough nutrition. I told her to eat well and rest. She looked at me incredulously, and then slowly stood up to leave. An invisible hand seemed to be moving her, causing her to sway her skeletal hips this way and that like seaweed. The giant sea spider was lurking in the background, crawling slowly across the deep ocean floor, waiting to sink its spindly legs into the leaf and tear her to little shreds while she went drifting along the ocean for another hundred miles.

12

Dhruv squinted at the client whose wart got bigger and bigger as he spoke.

'We don't have a budget for Paris!' he croaked. 'Can't you Photoshop the Eiffel Tower and shoot at Prasad Studios?'

Dhruv was speechless. He hadn't expected the stingy old client to approve a Paris budget but he hadn't imagined this either. He imagined spending three days with Anjolie in Kodambakkam and tried to come up with something better.

'Let's shoot at the Taj Mahal.'

'Taj Mahal?'

'Yes, let's substitute the Taj Mahal for the Eiffel Tower. That would make the jeans more desi. That's what you want, right?'

'Correct.' The client nodded his big bald head and stared at Dhruv through enormous eyes but Dhruv knew he was doing the math in his head.

'We can't Photoshop the Eiffel Tower! Either we shoot in Agra or I write you another commercial.'

Normally the client would have asked him to write another commercial. Write two more commercials, he would have said. But Dhruv had a sneaky feeling he liked the idea of the camera zooming in on the woman's butt.

'Okay,' he said.

'Okay, I write you another commercial?'

'Okay, we shoot in Agra.'

Dhruv's smile crept back to his face. He sipped his coffee. It was sweet and milky and lacked a shot of rum. He drank it in one big gulp and left the client's office. It was hot outside. He looked for his car in the parking lot. The cars stood still. The sky stood still. Clouds sailed past like ships in the distance and he thought of Anjolie. She must be standing in the balcony on one leg. Or she must be sitting cross-legged and painting her toenails. Or, he thought, getting into his car and starting the engine, she must be saluting the late afternoon sun. His eccentric girlfriend always brought a smile to his face.

That's what she was, he thought, and his smile widened on one side of his face, revealing a perfectly lopsided grin to a passer-by who looked into the panoramic windshield. She was his girlfriend.

Dhruv took a right at Gemini Circle and entered Cathedral Road. He drove past Woodlands on the right and found himself in a traffic jam outside Stella Maris. Everywhere there were cars and girls, cars and girls, cars and girls. If there were fewer cars and more girls, he thought, grinning from ear to ear, what a beautiful world it would be. A girl in a bright floral dress crossed the few inches of road between him and the next car. A waif with a baby in her arms tapped at his window and stretched out her skinny brown arms. A little boy in torn brown shorts was trying to clean his windshield, making it dirtier with every wipe. He rolled down the window and placed some coins in the waif's hand and when the boy came rushing to the window, he gave him his sandwich.

He was that age when his dad moved out. Let's take a breath of fresh air, his mom told him that unusually cloudy evening, and took him to the Theosophical Society. This banyan tree was grown from an offshoot of the banyan tree under which Buddha was enlightened, she said, looking at the aerial roots. Now you'll be enlightened too.

Whether it was the Adyar banyan tree that did it that day or the mammoth joints that he smoked in the forests of the IIT campus where he studied engineering, Dhruv had always felt quite enlightened.

It all began on his thirteenth birthday when he came home from school and found a parcel lying on the doorstep postmarked Dusseldorf. He was thrilled to bits because he knew it was from his much older German cousin whom he adored. He had last seen him when he was six years old on his only German vacation and now, seven years later, he had remembered his birthday!

But he hadn't remembered his birthday. In fact, he had no clue when his birthday was. It was his girlfriend's birthday when Hans was having dinner at the Chanakya Indian Restaurant in Koenigsallee and thought of his young Indian cousin. He had last seen the boy when he was six years old. And when he sang carols at a Christmas dinner, he had looked like a psychedelic rockstar in the bud. I wonder how he's doing, *der bubi*, thought Hans, biting into the spicy hot chicken, and decided to send him a gift.

Dhruv held the parcel in his hands. It seemed like there was a magazine inside. It must be *National Geographic*, he thought. He often daydreamed that someone would gift him a lifetime's subscription to the *National Geographic* and he would receive the canary yellow magazine at his doorstep every month. (A year later, he would dream of a lifetime's subscription to *Playboy*.) He tore open the parcel. Inside there were records of a band called *The Velvet Underground*.

This is to split open your mind. Love, Hans.

What split open Dhruv's mind was 'The Gift' inside the gift. Over eight minutes long, the song was mixed in such a way that a short story could be heard on the left speaker and a rock instrumental on the right. That weekend when he went to stay with his dad, he told him that he wanted to become a songwriter. His father bought him his first guitar. He would strum along to popular tunes while he stayed with his mom during the week and then play them to his dad over the weekend. He could never figure out why his parents were separated. They still did the crossword together. But why were they separated, he wondered, as if there was a comma between them?

'We grew out of it,' his mom told him years later when he was in college, 'and we stopped having sex.'

That day he resolved that if he were ever to fall in love with a girl and marry her, he would never separate because they stopped having sex. Tulsi and he hadn't had sex in several months. She didn't want to try for a baby any more. That's it, she had said when he tried to kiss her, the next time we have sex it must be because we can't keep our hands off each other.

But he didn't miss the sex, not with his wife. He had been meeting Anjolie every day and *they* couldn't keep their hands off each other.

—

I saw Tulsi at the supermarket. I was throwing handfuls of beans and carrots into a plastic bag and I spotted her carefully selecting a perfect red apple, a plump yellow banana and two bright oranges. I had never seen anyone choose apples with such care and it was only when I went up to her to say hello that I realized why.

'Doctor! What a surprise! You come here?'

'I have to do my grocery shopping too, you know. I can see that you take great care to do yours.'

'Oh, these!' she said, laughing. 'I'm choosing them for a painting. Dhruv does the grocery shopping usually.'

'Lucky you! It's an awfully boring task.'

'He says it's meditative. I think it's an excuse to buy loads of junk food.'

I thought it was an excuse to meet Anjolie but I didn't tell her that. A few weeks earlier, I had seen them coming out of a restaurant on TTK Road, a small Malayali joint that serves beer. They looked drunk in the middle of the afternoon but of course it had nothing to do with the beer.

I said goodbye to Tulsi and went on with the rest of my shopping. I wondered how she would react when she found out about Anjolie. Would she be hurt and angry? Would she leave Dhruv? Would she tell herself that it was just sex and forgive him? Or would she want him more than ever after finding him in the arms of a gorgeous woman?

Tulsi ambled to the cash counter with a basketful of fruit and a spring in her step. She hummed a soft tune as she paid, and then disappeared through the glass doors of the supermarket.

Rodin was dead for over eighty years. Kundera was living for under eighty years. In 1970, when access to his work was banned in Czechoslovakia, Kundera was reduced to writing an astrology column under a fictitious name. That's like an artist working in advertising, Tulsi thought, sitting in her red and white cubicle on the fifth floor of a corporate building on Mount Road.

She reread the brief for a hibiscus shampoo. She read the ingredients on the bottle. Magnesium Sulfate, Sodium Thiosulfate, Sodium Olefin Sulfonate, Sodium Citrate, Sodium Benzoate, Alkyl Sodium Sulfate, Alkyl Benzene Sulfonate, Sodium Chloride, fragrance and water. Where was the hibiscus?

The scarlet, trumpet-shaped flowers were painted on the bottle along with the brand name and a model with gleaming black hair. She opened the bottle. It smelt like a scented candle. She looked out of the window at Mount Road below her. There were buses, auto-rickshaws and cars and people and people and they were slowly fading away. It was six o'clock in late October. The sun was already setting and the fluorescent street lamps were yet to burn. Inside, it was still and the stale air-conditioned air crept into her pores.

A bearded market researcher drifted into Creative and sat next to Paul, the junior copywriter with a tangled mop of curls.

'Your target audience wears nylex saris and uses talcum powder,' he said.

Tara cringed in her seat. She wore talcum powder, ever so gently dusted over her round face so that nobody would find out. It keeps the oil away, she had confided to Tulsi one afternoon in the ladies' room, and makes my skin two shades lighter.

'Your target audience eats tiffin for dinner: idli, dosa, upma, pongal…' he went on.

Nobody cringed. They all ate hearty dinners with oodles of rice and chapatti after having a couple of beers in the evening.

'Now I'm hungry, yaar,' said an art director looking up from his artwork. 'Let's order mini idlis from Saravana Bhavan.'

'Your TA will try any new fairness cream that comes into the market for half the price.'

Paul said he needed to take a leak.

'Your TA will buy a sachet of fairness cream for twice the price without realizing that she's actually spending a hell of a lot more than she would on a tube.

'That's the market we have to tap,' he finally said with a satisfied smile.

Paul looked like he would explode.

Poor TA, Tulsi thought. Wearing those mottled nylex saris to save money and then splurging on sachets of fairness cream! Suddenly she felt claustrophobic. She went to the terrace to breathe. It was warm and there were pockets of shadow but the air was still. She lit a cigarette and thought about life before all this began. What was it like before advertising, before brands came into existence, when Nike was a goddess and not a shoe, when coke was a fuel and not a drink?

Suddenly the wind was in her face. It was everywhere – in the trees, in her skirt and in her expanding lungs. She felt stronger and more feminine. Her hair was blowing in the wind. Her short, straight hair was long now and curled at the ends. My hair has some spirit after all, she thought. I had to let it grow to find out.

Her mobile rang. It was Dhruv, reminding her that he was leaving for Agra that night.

'Will you be home before I leave?' he asked.

'I have to crack this hibiscus ad.'

'I've made dinner for you, sweetie, so finish up, come home and relax.'

'That was thoughtful, Dhruv. How long will you be gone?'

'A couple of days. It's a hectic schedule so don't wait for me to call.'

'You're going to see the Taj Mahal?'

'I'm shooting in front of the Taj, baby.'

Think of me when you're there, she wanted to say. She said goodbye and hung up. Agra was a quaint old city. It would be chill in October while here they were still waiting for the monsoon to cool the earth. She remembered the narrow winding streets and archaic red buildings. She remembered posing in front of the Taj with her family when she was little. One day when she was all grown up she would go there with her man, she had thought then, and pose for a photograph with an arm around him.

Tulsi stood on the terrace of the five-storied building under the first star that lit up the sky. It was a speck of silver, a tiny shimmer of hope in the darkening sky. She stood against the parapet wall, gazing at the Chennai skyline. Life was elsewhere, she thought.

Life was always elsewhere. Once she thought it was in a marketplace in a *National Geographic* magazine; another time she thought it was in the arms of Berliners when the wall fell; and when she went to Paris for her honeymoon, she thought it was in a cemetery alongside the graves of Jim

Morrison and Oscar Wilde. It had surely been on the walls of the Sorbonne in May '68, but life was never here. You could never catch it and say, here it is, this is life right here in my hand.

The neighbouring building with frosted glass windows and chocolate-brown paint stood seven storeys tall. And on a fifth storey, a pale yellow light made patterns on the glass. Life is in that room, she thought. She noticed a slow and steady movement on the glass, as if a couple inside were making love. But moments later when she looked at the window again, she realized it was the leaves of a plant on the windowsill. They were fluttering. The life she thought she had caught within the four walls of a room was in the leaves of a plant. And it was trapped in a pot.

She had one more hour to crack the ad. She went back downstairs and sat in front of her computer. She searched the word 'shampoo'. There was a film called *Shampoo* and video results for how to shampoo your hair. She searched the most searched words on the internet. In J it was jobs. In K it was J F K. In L it was lottery and love. She Googled more words. She Googled the word 'Google'. She read that the name 'Google' originated from a common misspelling of the word 'googol', which refers to the number represented by 1 followed by one hundred zeros.

There must be a googol ways to do this bloody ad and you know what, she said to herself, I'm not going to do even one of them. She looked around Creative. A copywriter sat at his desk whistling loudly. An art director, a pencil behind one ear, was gaping at the wall in front of him.

She strolled around the office. An account executive had put up something on his soft board. *One rule of action more important than all others consists of never doing anything that someone else can do for you.* An honest declaration for an AE, she thought.

Life is what happens to you, the media planner had written with a black marker pen on a white board, *while you're busy making other plans.*

Tulsi sauntered back to her desk and created a new Word file. She named it 'Googol ways to live your life' and typed out her resignation letter.

A super massive black hole would take a googol years to evaporate, her letter began, *but I have about fifty years left to live.* She finished her letter and emailed it to the creative head who was sitting three feet away from her. She shut down her computer and left the office. In the old days, when she imagined leaving advertising, she imagined herself snapping her notepad shut, putting her pencil down and walking out of the door. That was how Dhruv had left. But then these days there were computers and there was the internet and there were a googol ways to live a life.

———

Anjolie tied a strapless bra to a pair of thongs and threw it inside the overnight bag that lay on the floor with its zipper wide open. She packed her underwear first wherever she went; because she wore them first, she reasoned. She packed a pair of jeans, two full-sleeved tops and a nice warm sweater. She wrapped a newspaper around her Osho chappals and tossed them inside. She was done.

She would meet Dhruv in less than two hours and they would leave for Agra like honeymooners. Dhruv had carefully booked them on a different flight from the rest of the crew. So we can hold hands, he had said, sounding delighted. Suddenly she felt young and excited and guilty.

She told herself she wasn't doing anything wrong. After all, it was a legitimate shoot; she was the model and he was the writer and it was a jeans commercial. She left a note for her husband who wouldn't be home before she left. *Will miss you*, she scrawled on the back of an envelope and left it on the dining table.

She hated lying.

Something told her that her life would change forever. She had a sixth sense about things before they happened and she blamed it on twenty-five years of yoga. It was a side effect of meditation; you could feel things in your bones before they happened.

There was a part of her that wanted to beat it and run from it and never see Dhruv again but she knew that was not possible. She had signed a contract with the agency and they were shooting the next morning. They had work all day but their nights were free and Dhruv and she could explore Agra, explore each other. That was what frightened her.

She wrapped a black Kashmiri stole around herself and slipped into a pair of freshly ironed black linen pants. She swung her bag over her shoulder and ran down the stairs. There was a taxi waiting for her on the road. In twenty minutes she would be in the airport ready to fall into Dhruv's arms. But she was scared. She was scared that something was going to happen that hadn't happened before.

What am I going to do that I haven't already done, she asked herself. She had already given herself away, body and soul. She had cried while making love and she had cried while making the bed afterwards. And every time they made love, she changed the sheets, stripping the guilt clean and covering the dirty mattress with new linen.

She had butterflies in her stomach. She shook her head.

I'm going to wreck my journey before it has even begun. I'm just going to leave this feeling back in Madras and deal with it when I come back, she told herself and looked out of the window. Everything slowed down and the taxi stopped at a signal in Guindy behind a column of cars. On the pavement, street women had lined up in rows around a water pump with plastic water pots. What bright colours they came in, she thought, looking at the shocking pinks, violets and fluorescent greens. The women stood on the pavement unwearyingly, waiting to pump the water. And when they finally pumped the water into the fantastic pots, lifted them up, placed them on their hips and carried them seamlessly, they looked like they were carrying babies to the fair. The pots looked alive on the street – unlike the brand-new ones on the window of the Park Hotel – as if each one had a story of its own, a bittersweet tale fabricated with blood, sweat and plastic. The taxi moved. The pavement with the pots disappeared. Soon she would be on a flight and the butterflies would disappear like the city beneath her and she would be on a cross-country flight to paradise. And when Dhruv put his arm around her, she would feel his weight crushing her body and she would feel heavy, unbearably heavy, and full of life.

Tulsi was out of the office. She was standing on Mount Road looking at the buses that went past with people hanging out of the door. She felt free for the first time in years. She had started working when she was nineteen. She had given the best years of her life to advertising. Now she was free.

Suddenly she felt an overwhelming desire to go to Marina Beach. She used to go there with her brother and cousins when she was little, and once, years ago, she had climbed the lighthouse and looked at the sea from there. The lighthouse was so tall then. But she was a big girl now and things had changed.

She called her friends and made a quick beach plan but they weren't so enthusiastic about going to Marina Beach.

'Are you nuts?' Kavita said on the phone. 'It's bloody crowded. Let's hit ECR Road instead.'

'But we can get sundal and corn,' Tulsi begged.

And so they went, two boys and three girls, her best friends from her college days.

The lighthouse had surely shrunk, she thought when she reached the beach, and the population had exploded. The sundal looked suspicious and the corn was dry. They walked along the long stretch of sand that led to the sea and stood facing the ocean. The water sprayed on their faces. They drew faces in the sand that the ocean wiped away in seconds.

A little boy came up to them selling balloons and her friends told him to take a walk. Do we look like we play with balloons, Sanjay said, and Tulsi ran behind the little balloon boy and bought five bright balloons with a ten-rupee note. She gave one to each of her friends.

'This,' she said, 'is to remind you that we are still young and free.'

'I'm free, honey,' said Kavita who was still single. 'Need I remind you that you're not, *Frau* Schumacher?'

Tulsi wasn't amused. She was looking at the waves, imagining two bright balloons tied together for life, one for her and one for Dhruv, flying above the ocean, into the sky.

13

Today is Diwali – the Indian Christmas, as an English friend of mine said when I was living in London and looking longingly at the October sky for skyrockets and sparkling shapes. I wake up to a cacophony, shower and delete half a million messages that are eating up my phone. Mother is the first to call at six a.m. Happy Deepavali, she says. Udambukku onnum illamairikiyono? Literally translated, this means: Hope you don't have anything in your body. 'I am naked, ma, how did you guess,' I say, teasing her. But what she means is: Hope you don't have an ailment in your body. The last time she called I was running a temperature of 102 and rushing to the clinic with a pocketful of Crocin. I am fine, ma, I say, and she starts talking about one of my sister's colleagues. Clever boy, she keeps repeating. Looks like Kamal Haasan. In which movie, I ask. He looks different in every movie. You are always playing the fool, she admonishes me and gives the phone to dad who is terribly excited about a cricket match he saw on big screen. I have a half-hour conversation with Maya,

who goes on to enumerate the reasons why I should take a
vacation in Sunnyvale and spend my afternoons sitting in
her backyard eating blueberries.

I miss my family. I remember how grandmother would
wake us up at four in the morning on Deepavali and massage
our heads with sesame oil. We would spring out of bed,
bleary-eyed and eager, waiting to wear our new pavadais
and burst crackers. Once, Maya kept an atom bomb on
our windowsill to scare me. She would peel the paper from
the cracker fuse, light it in her hand and throw it before it
burst while I prayed for her life and distracted myself with
sparklers.

I have no appointments today, no surgeries. The clinic is
running with two Christian nurses and a Muslim watchman
who doubles up as receptionist. The rest of the staff is at
home celebrating Deepavali with their loved ones. The air
is thick with poisonous fumes and if I step outside and don't
breathe, it feels like a foggy day in Delhi. I am eighteen
years old, standing with a basketful of dreams in Connaught
Place. Shanti is standing next to me, my dearest friend who
came all the way from Madras with me. We are standing on
the invisible pavement gaping at the fog because we have
never seen anything like it. This looks like heaven with
headlights, she says. Because all you can see are the hazy
lights circling around, everything else is covered in mist and
it does feel like heaven.

A string of loud bangs shakes me from my reverie. My
neighbour is bursting a ten-thousand wala on the street. I
go inside and shut the door. There is a large unopened box
lying on the floor, filled with firecrackers. I look at them
and think of the child labourers in Sivakasi who made them,
sitting cross-legged and stuffing gunpowder into tubes with

their tiny little hands. Do *they* get to take home free crackers to burst on Deepavali?

I miss Sid. The last time he called, I was in surgery and when I called back the number, it was a phone booth in Rio de Janeiro. Sometimes I wonder if I am fooling myself into believing I'm in a relationship. I go to my room and sit at my desk by the window. I look at photographs of Sid and me at the beach. I open a Word file and bring my fingers to the keyboard. Once again, my travel writer is travelling and lets me do the writing alone. Does he know that it is Deepavali today in India?

I open the window and the foul air enters my nostrils. In the distance, a rocket takes off from an empty bottle. I wish I could take off like that. But I would need a propellant stronger than gunpowder packed tight with little hands to uproot me from here and send me into the sky.

———

It wasn't spontaneous.

They had talked about kissing each other on the lips before. It was after watching *Belle de Jour* that they finally did it. Zubeida had the idea of course, but it was Seema who took the initiative. She brought her face close to Zubeida's and closed her eyes. Zubeida held Seema's face with her cushiony hands and put her soft lips against hers. When Zubeida opened her mouth, Seema was quick to taste her tongue and explore the depths of her delicious mouth.

And so they kissed, Zubeida with her eyes open and Seema with her eyes closed. It was like drinking water after a long day in the sun. It moistened their lips and quenched their thirst. It was provocative and it was profound and it was very long. It was the most beautiful kiss in their lives and would always be.

They wouldn't kiss again.

When it was over, they giggled. Her youngest son woke up from his nap and Zubeida grabbed him and ran back to her flat to make egg dosas for the boys, who would be home any minute. Her cheeks were flushed, her lips were red and slightly swollen, and her eyes glowed like fireflies. She had never enjoyed making dosas so much before.

She looked out of the kitchen window and saw the boys walking home with enormous bags on their shoulders. They carry so many books to school, she thought, and the oldest is barely nine. And look at her third one, just three years old and walking behind his brothers with a huge bag! The poor creatures. Their bags are bigger than they are and I never noticed before.

She opened the door and they ran in and threw their bags on the stained mosaic floor. She served them dosas with mutton curry and watched them eat. Her eldest son Nabil pulled out a Five Star from his pocket and broke it into four tiny pieces. He gave one to each of his brothers and popped the last little piece into his mouth. Zubeida looked at him and her eyes welled up.

'I'm sorry, ammi,' he said. 'Don't cry! I didn't know you like chocolate too!'

'No, my love,' she said, 'I don't.' I didn't know *you* like chocolate, that you bring it home from school and share it with your little brothers.

The doorbell rang. Seema walked in with a bowl of firni.

'Today is a special day,' she said and placed it on the dining table.

Zubeida went to the kitchen to bring serving bowls and

they sat around the dining table. Zubeida propped up her youngest, who was almost two years old, on two pillows over a chair and he dipped his spoon into the firni and made slurping noises. Nabil finished his bowl and thanked Seema. When the boys had finished and left the table, Seema looked at Zubeida, her eyes sparkling.

'This will keep me going,' she said.

'Me too, Seem. What are we watching tomorrow?'

'*Life Is Beautiful.*'

'It certainly is,' said Zubeida, flashing her radiant smile.

When Seema left, Zubeida watched *Mr Bean* cartoons with the boys. When the show ended, Nabil did an imitation for his younger brothers. Zubeida laughed. She had not realized how talented her son was. She had not realized many things.

While the younger boys played hide-and-seek, Nabil went to the dining table to do his science homework. Zubeida wiped the table and sat next to him, looking into the notebook. She was back in the chemistry lab on her last day of school. She could smell hydrogen sulphide in a test tube but it didn't smell like rotten eggs. It smelt masculine. It smelt like Sandeep would smell now, she thought, not like her husband who smelt of mutton and sweat. But if she were to see Sandeep walking down the street, she wouldn't recognize him. How would he look now, she wondered. Would he have a moustache? Would he have a beard? He would be clean shaven, she decided, like a male model in a cologne commercial.

And with that thought, she smelt amber and peppermint and suddenly she smelt rotten eggs and came back to her tiny apartment in Triplicane with bottle-green windows and peeling paint.

Nabil finished his homework and joined the neighbourhood boys in a cricket game. They drew stumps on the concrete wall and played with an old bat and tennis ball. I wish I could get them a cricket ball and a new bat, she thought. She went to the kitchen and served herself mutton curry and finished the last greasy dosa, standing in the kitchen and licking her fingers clean. Her fingernails looked glossy, the red nail polish reflected the light from the window and in her shining fingernails, Zubeida saw the boys playing cricket with a shiny red cricket ball.

When Zubeida came to see me at seven that evening, she had a culpable look on her face. She isn't supposed to be here, I thought, that's why she looks guilty.

'Doctor, I waited one whole hour to see you and I don't have any time left. Mustafa doesn't know I'm here.'

'What is it?' I asked anxiously.

'Can you give me some birth control pills?'

I heaved a sigh of relief. For a moment I had been afraid for her, thinking she was in some sort of trouble. I wrote out a prescription and gave it to her and started explaining how she should take them.

'Start your first pack of pills on the first day of your period...' I began.

'Doctor, you have to give them to me. I can't go to a pharmacy and buy them. It's forbidden in my religion. If Mustafa were to find out...'

'All right,' I said. 'I should have a few sample packs. You can take them.'

I looked in my drawer. All I could dig out were two pocket-sized packs of the miraculous drug that had changed the lives of women across the world. When the FDA announced in May 1960 that Enovid, a prescription drug that had been used for several years to treat menstrual disorders, was safe to use as an oral contraceptive, millions of women were given the freedom to make a choice they didn't have earlier. And now, half a century later, there were still women across the world who were left without the most fundamental of choices.

'I'll be back for more,' she said, running to the door. 'And thank you, doctor, thank you!'

That's how I started seeing Zubeida regularly. She would drop in every couple of months to take birth control pills from me and we would chat. She hid them in a box in the kitchen and took them when she washed the dishes at night. She wasn't obsessed about having a girl any more. She had four beautiful boys and they were growing up quickly.

Her husband had allowed her to go for a computer class down the road. The teacher was a woman, she explained. She saw the World Wide Web for the first time. I had only read about it before but now I've seen it, she said excitedly. They were going to buy a computer soon, she said, second hand. 'Then I'll navigate all over the world.'

—

Megha peered into the world map in her daughter's geography textbook. Africa looked like an ice-cream cone. She imagined biting into the rainbow-flavoured blob. She had licked off Morocco and was now sinking her teeth into Algeria and Libya.

'Mama,' said Barkha, breaking her train of thought. 'When I grow up I want to be an explorer.'

She wondered how much money explorers made and

who paid them to explore. And what on earth did they explore? It would be better to be a programmer. There were thousands of jobs for programmers and even she knew the names of software companies. Wipro, Infosys, Microsoft.

'What did you want to be when you were a little girl?' Barkha asked, gaping at her with wide brown eyes.

'Teri ma,' she said. Your mother. And if she did that job well, her purpose in life would be fulfilled.

'And Bijli's and Titli's,' Barkha said.

'And Bijli's and Titli's.'

'And nobody else's!'

'And nobody else's!'

Yes indeed, Megha said to herself; I need to make sure my three little girls grow up and stand on their own feet so they break free from this cycle of bonded labour. *Dowry. Marriage. Labour. Birth. Dowry. Marriage. Labour. Birth.*

'See, mama! There's a country called Kiribati!' said Barkha laughing.

'Sounds like dal-baati!' said Megha, peering at the widely scattered islands in the Pacific.

'Mama, why are only you cooking for everybody? Chachi and dadi never go into the kitchen. It's so nice when you sit with me while I do my homework.'

It's so nice when I sit with you. It's so nice when I sit, thought Megha, as every muscle in her body hurt. Soon she would have to get up and go to the kitchen and cook up a storm. She picked up her littlest, Titli, and took her downstairs to feed her dinner. Her husband was just entering the house so she put her down and went to make tea. Suddenly her eyes filled with tears. She boiled the tea for what seemed like hours, roasted some almonds and put them into a bowl and carried it to the living room with the pot of tea. It was scalding hot. I should just topple it over somebody, she thought suddenly. But who?

And then she did it, without another thought, she toppled the pot of tea over herself, scalding her hands and stomach and thighs. It scorched and singed and she would be bandaged up in bed for a week, sitting next to her little Barkha doing her homework, and somebody would have to go into the kitchen and do the cooking but it was not going to be her.

—

Another year was drawing to an end. Another calendar would be taken off the walls and tossed into a bin. It had been just four years since I moved back to Madras and so much had happened and yet so little. While Zubeida had embraced her life, Megha was still battling against all odds. Tulsi and Anjolie were revolving like planets around the same sun. Sid had been gone so long that I felt as lonely as I did that New Year's Day when I walked into the airport with a trolley full of suitcases.

It was all leading to something, I thought, and this time I would not sit back and watch like a spectator in the dark as I did the day Zubeida and Megha delivered together; this time I would play my part.

While the storm was brewing in and around our lives, another one had been brewing, quite literally. Colossal forces that had been building up deep in the earth for hundreds of years were released, unzipping the ocean bed and unleashing a succession of devastating tsunamis along the Indian Ocean, killing over two hundred thousand people in eleven countries.

It was calm on Marina Beach that Sunday morning. There was anticipation in the air with Christmas holidays having just begun. Children were playing cricket, adults were going for their morning walk and fishermen were preparing their nets for the day's catch. All of a sudden, the sea receded and a gargantuan killer wave lashed at them, taking them by surprise, and each time the wave came back, it took more lives with it.

Without exception, I have gone to the beach every Sunday morning. I love the sea, and this is my way of unwinding after the long week. That day, when I was about to leave the house, the clinic called. A young woman with an undetected ectopic pregnancy had come in with a ruptured Fallopian tube and I rushed to the clinic to perform an emergency surgery. I saved her life and she saved mine.

But I felt helpless towards the hundreds of people who had lost their lives and homes around me, mostly in fishing villages along the coast. I had my work cut out for me at the clinic. But as the scenes replayed on television and people talked about it in the papers, in websites, in homes, I couldn't help but imagine myself on the beach when the sea let loose a hundred-foot wave. My nightmares came back and understandably they were mostly of the sea, with me looking around helplessly as people died and their bodies floated about like paper boats.

Seven for a secret
never to be told

14

I come home at ten in the night and leave at six in the morning when I have surgery scheduled, which gives me eight hours to myself to read, write, eat and sleep in that order. I'm thankful that I practise a profession I love. I encounter several women and get a peek into their lives and their heads and I can't think of any profession more interesting other than perhaps the auto-rickshaw driver who picks up people and takes them around this stunningly diverse city while getting a glimpse into their lives.

My profession involves psychology and surgery, internal medicine and counselling, all in a day's work. The surgery is taken care of by the left side of my brain, the logical, sequential and analytical part automatically cuts through tissues, resectioning, litigating, grafting and suturing, but it is the right side of my brain that struggles – to be intuitive, holistic and subjective, to look at the whole instead of the parts.

Let us ruminate on the whole. Zubeida Zainuddin is the mother of four young boys, Megha Jhunjhunwala of three young girls. As much as I counsel her not to have a fourth, my instinct tells me she will be back in this room with an inflated tummy and a shrunken frame and a haemoglobin count of six. Tulsi is dabbling in art while Anjolie is dabbling in her husband and something tells me that I will be summoned to resection, graft and suture their psychological wounds.

—

The King stabbed the Queen and she lay on the table, bleeding next to the Jack. There were seven diamonds, five spades and two beating hearts.

It was a King top and a Queen top in a poker game. Dhruv had the King and Tulsi had the Queen. When she saw his King, she threw her cards on the table and stormed out of the room. She had just lost a million dollars.

'All is fair in love and cards. You can give me the million dollars in kind,' he teased, running behind her.

'I'm never playing with you again! You have the devil's luck!'

He followed her to the bedroom.

She fell on the bed and started crying. 'I have a strange feeling that I'm losing you,' she said softly.

'You're not losing me, silly, you're losing *to* me! A million dollars to be precise. And when you sell your paintings in Paris next month, you can pay me.'

With interest, he added and kissed her. He wanted to make love to her more than ever and when he did, he thought, the guilt would melt away. She kissed him back and saw his face through the tears clouding her eyes. He looks like a god, she thought, my husband looks like a living god and I've been pushing him away for so long. She unbuttoned his jeans.

'Where are those orange-flavoured condoms that you got at the client meeting?'

'Are you sure you want to?'

'Yes. Where are those condoms?'

'I don't have them.'

'You don't have them? But you said the client gave you dozens of packs.'

He had used the last two with Anjolie that morning and she had joked about how he would smell of oranges all day.

'He did. But I threw them away because... because I thought they'd expired.'

'What? Condoms have a shelf life of four or five years!'

'How come you're so interested in condoms all of a sudden?'

'Because I want to use them, obviously.'

'The orange turns you on?'

'No, moron, you turn me on but I want to use a condom while doing it.'

His phone beeped. Dhruv read the message and said he'd be back and went out in a tearing hurry.

I need to tell him I want him, she thought. I also need to tell him that I don't want to get pregnant. She knew the probability of her getting pregnant was dim. It was like a Royal Flush in a poker game, but it was possible. She had taken countless pregnancy tests in the past, longing to see a second line, sometimes closing her eyes for the full three minutes and willing for it to appear like she used to will for a rainbow to appear in the sky when she was a little girl.

But she had grown up now. She didn't want to get pregnant any more. She wanted to adopt a baby girl and she wanted to tell Dhruv about it. She wanted to tell him so many things. Most of all she wanted to tell him how much she loved him, but he was gone.

He was in a different world these days, and in that world there was someone else. She was certain of it now. From the way he had grabbed his phone and rushed out to make a call, she was sure. But who could it be, she wondered. Whoever she was, there must be something so captivating about her that Dhruv had fallen like a coin, his head against the ground. And then she remembered the woman in the red dress whom she met at the jazz concert and the look on Dhruv's face when he introduced her. It was her.

Tulsi undressed and stood in front of the mirror. Her shoulders were sinewy, her belly was smooth and her legs were muscular. All that running finally shows on my body, she thought. It shows on my face. It looks like a face that has seen miles. She had been running all these years, running and running in search of herself, and now that she had finally found it, it was trapped in two dimensions on a looking glass.

She massaged under-eye cream around her eyes and on her cheeks. She closed her eyes and massaged them slowly. Her face was radiant in the twilight and when she opened her eyes again, they twinkled like the first two stars to appear in the sky. She touched her breasts; they were firm yet soft. Her nipples responded to her touch. She tucked her hair behind her ears. It fell beyond her shoulders and she looked more beautiful than she had looked in all her life. I seem to have finally found myself, she thought, at the age of thirty-five.

Or have I found my *other* self?

She lay on the bed and waited for Dhruv. It seemed like hours had gone by and there was no sign of him. She lay naked, looking at the square white ceiling, trying not to think of the other woman. The rotating fan looked like

a translucent circle. If she were to look at the situation
geometrically, she would be an incidence. She would be a
line contained in a plane. The other woman was an incidence
too; maybe she had a greater impact at the present but she
was an incidence nevertheless, and together they were
coincidences in Dhruv's life.

She looked at her unfinished painting on the easel. It was a
cubist work of two women in monochromatic browns, greys
and blacks with only their eyes in colour. She had broken up
the two women and reassembled them from a multitude of
view points and now they were reduced to basic geometric
parts on the picture plane. One of the women would have
to rise beyond the plane and appear as a line, and then she
realized that *that* was the line she was willing to appear, not
the rainbow and certainly not the one in the pregnancy kit.
It was herself.

———

It was a month since the day she had left for Agra with
butterflies in her stomach, butterflies that she eventually
abandoned on a pavement in Guindy with pink and violet
plastic pots. It was exactly a month from that day that she saw
the purple line. It was the same line that she had looked for
when she was trying to have a baby with Neel. It was staring
at her on the other side of the window of the pregnancy test,
but it had a different face.

She was certain the baby was Dhruv's. She even knew
when it was conceived. It was their last night in Agra and
she had had the awful feeling that it was their last night ever,
but he held her and told her it wasn't, that they would see
each other again. The night before, they had made love until
the morning; she told him he was her rock star, that she

was his groupie, that she would make love to him anytime, anywhere; all he had to do was call her name. And he called her name again and again and again. When they finally fell asleep with the sound of the birds, she had that dream, that terrible dream.

It's midnight. She knows it is midnight because she hears a grandfather clock chime twelve times. She is walking on a deserted road and she wonders where the grandfather clock could possibly be. It must be hanging on a tree, she decides; after all it's easy to drill a nail into a tree trunk. She goes in search of the grandfather clock and she is lost. There are cockerels everywhere and they are flapping their wings. This is odd, she thinks, this is terribly odd. You will meet the prince at twelve past twelve, says a cockerel and flies off. She looks around for the cockerel and sees a bare-chested man wearing a ruby red crown. He looks beautiful, and she realizes it is Dhruv. He takes her in his arms but when she looks up at him, it is not Dhruv. At least, not *her* Dhruv. His eyes are not brown but dirty green and his hair is not brown but bright orange and when he opens his mouth to kiss her, his teeth are missing.

That was when she woke up screaming and he held her and whispered that it was all right, everything was all right, they still had one more night together. She looked at his face in the dark and she was so relieved to see his face, to see his brown eyes and shaggy brown hair, his perfect white teeth and lopsided smile. She put her arms around him and fell asleep but soon it was time for them to leave. It was dawn and they needed some shots in the early morning light.

When they came back that evening, tired and aching after two days of working in the sun and two nights of constant lovemaking, they fell into each other's arms and made love again. Then they showered and drank five big Kingfishers between them and went to Zorba the Buddha, where she had a delightfully green okra curry and he a ruddy paneer butter masala which they polished off with a dozen rotis. Then they walked back to their hotel room and fell into bed. That was the night she conceived. She told him how they had been trying to have a baby and he told her how they had been trying too and they supposed that it was very safe to make love just once without a layer of latex in the way. That's when she conceived.

She had lain awake in Dhruv's arms till the morning light crept through the curtains and showered his hair with its translucent light. He was sleeping with a smile on his face and she cried. She would never see that smile at sunrise again. And then his phone alarm rang and they grabbed their bags and rushed to the airport. The cab driver thought they were honeymooners and he talked to them non-stop; he told them how lovers who visited the Taj Mahal stayed in love forever, like Shah Jahan and Mumtaz Mahal. Didn't Mumtaz Mahal die, she wanted to ask, and leave Shah Jahan heartbroken for the rest of his life?

Now she was back in her apartment, sitting in front of her laptop and reading *Le Monde* online. She would abort the baby and never see Dhruv again. Unlike Mumtaz Mahal, she wouldn't die in childbirth but in *not* giving birth.

She made up her mind and started to shut down the system. A warning message came up on the screen. 'Terminating a process can cause undesired results including loss of data and system instability. The process will not be given a chance to save its state or data before it is terminated. Are you sure you want to terminate?'

There were only two choices: yes and no.

The doorbell rang twice in quick succession. That was the last time it would ring like that, she thought and opened the door. Dhruv stepped inside and took her in his arms.

'You have the baby,' he said, 'and we'll start all over again.'

'Are you crazy? I know you don't want to leave Tulsi. I know you love her. Maybe not like this but I know you love her. And what about Neel?'

'This is insane. I've been trying to have a baby with Tulsi forever and we've tried everything!'

'And I've been trying to have a baby with Neel!'

They began to kiss. She would never see him again, she decided as her lips sank into his. Her heart would bleed and she would let it bleed; it would be the biggest performance of her life but she would feel the pain and cross over to another state of consciousness.

It would be easier to let him go now that the decision had been made. That which does not kill us makes us stronger, she repeated Nietzsche's words in her head. She would pick up the pieces of her life and go on. She loved Neel. Maybe she wasn't in love with Neel. But she loved him. As for Dhruv, she was in love with Dhruv but did she love him? And did *he* love her?

She plucked an imaginary chrysanthemum from an imaginary plant and picked out the petals one by one. *Il m'aime un peu, beaucoup, passionnément, à la folie, pas du tout. Il m'aime un peu, beaucoup, passionnément, à la folie, pas du tout. Il m'aime un peu, beaucoup, passionnément, à la folie.* The last petal dropped to the floor.

Il m'aime à la folie, she said to herself.

'What are you saying, sweetheart?' he asked and pulled her towards him.

She thought of the tree that falls in a forest when there is no one around to hear it fall. She had always wondered if it would make a sound. It certainly would, she concluded as she fell into his arms for the last time. It would make a sound loud and clear – like his heartbeat.

———

This is what she needed me for, the beautiful damsel who had mastered her emotions and conquered her fears and performed harrowing pieces in front of spectators around the world. This is what she needed me for and she didn't know it when she came to me the first time. Now here she was in my consultation room, planning an abortion.

'I have to get up from here and go back to my husband like nothing happened,' she said.

I had no doubt that she could. She was very capable of waking up from a full-blown D&C and walking back home. In fact, she didn't even need anaesthesia. She could undergo the whole procedure with her eyes open. I wrote out some routine tests. I needed to confirm that it was an intrauterine pregnancy before I did the procedure. For that she would have to wait two more weeks. She winced. I told her to come back with the tests in two weeks. Then we'll do it straightaway, I promised.

I couldn't believe it could end like this. This time there must be something I can do, I thought. When Megha gave birth to her third girl child and Zubeida to her fourth boy, I knew it would be unethical if I did something. But this time there must be *something* I could do.

She came back in exactly two weeks with the tests. It was an intrauterine pregnancy and I explained that I would be using an abortion pill to expel the contents of the uterus. I told her that the combination of mifepristone and vaginal misoprostol could end most pregnancies in about four hours.

'That's it,' I said. 'You can drive back home and you'll start to bleed shortly after. That way you can be at home when you're cramping and bleeding.'

She looked relieved and grabbed the medicine from my hands.

'Alternatively,' I said, looking into her kaleidoscopic eyes, 'you could wait here for four hours.'

'You mean I can do it here?'

'No, I mean you can do it four hours later but you can sit here and think about not doing it.'

'I'm confused, doctor.'

'That's a good start,' I said. 'Confusion is a very good place to begin.'

'What do you mean, doctor?'

'You can sit here for the next four hours, outside my consultation room, and think about it. It's four-thirty now and I'll be here till eight-thirty. And if you still want to take them, I'll give you the pills at eight-thirty.'

'But…'

'But you and your husband could have a beautiful baby in nine months and he doesn't need to know it's not his.'

'But…'

'But it would be a great big lie. And it would be yours to live with. What he doesn't know isn't going to hurt him. Besides, you do know that flesh-and-blood is an illusion, don't you? DNA is not an emotion; it's an acid, like LSD.'

'Well, yes.'

'How many men have you loved?'

Anjolie smiled.

'Do you have their DNA? How many times have you met

someone and felt something for them and you hardly even know them, yet it's felt like you've known them all your life? Do you think you have the same DNA?'

Anjolie shook her head.

'Just sit in my waiting room and think for four hours. That's all I ask. You'll see lots of women, some of them might be really fat in their last trimester. Don't let *that* influence your decision.'

Anjolie laughed and left the room. Eight months later she delivered a beautiful baby boy.

'What if he becomes a musician,' she whispered to me. 'Won't Neel wonder where he got the musical genes from? Neither of us can sing to save our lives!'

'That only happens in Hollywood. In India, boys end up doing what their fathers do.'

They named their son Siddhartha. He has a mop of shaggy brown hair and a lopsided grin and he can draw molecular formulae in his colouring book.

—

Tulsi told me how her life changed the moment she saw her face. It was those big black eyes on that tiny body that did it. The minute she looked into them, she knew she was hers. What is she doing here, she wondered, in this strange home with a hundred other babies, when she should be with me? But she had to wait a whole day before she could take her home. That day was the longest in her life and she spent that night dreaming that she was a caregiver in the adoption home.

When they finally brought her home, weighing five-and-a-quarter kilos at seven months, she was the happiest woman in the world. Her daughter was finally home.

PRIYAMVADA N. PURUSHOTHAM

They named her Tanya. Little Tanya couldn't turn over on the day she came home. She could barely hold up her head. But within a week she was rolling around the bed. In a month she began to crawl. Her first word was 'papa'. Because it's easier to say papa than mama, Tulsi told me.

'Was language created by men?' she asked me, smiling. 'It's so much easier to say pa than ma.'

I laughed.

'But seriously, doctor, ma is a nasal sound, isn't it more difficult to utter?'

'I do believe language was created by men,' I said, 'but men were created by women.'

We laughed together. It was delightful to see Tulsi like this. She had come to me to get an intrauterine device. She told me that Dhruv and she didn't want more babies and when they were ready for another one, they would adopt again.

'But it would have to be a boy,' she said.

According to the Indian Adoption Act, you cannot adopt two girls or two boys; if you have a boy you can only adopt a girl, if you have a girl you can only adopt a boy.

I told her to call me when her next menstrual cycle started and come in for the insertion. I wrote out some routine tests and explained the fifteen-minute procedure.

'And Dhruv?' I asked. 'How is he doing?'

'Little T has him wrapped around her finger. All she has to do is flash her toothless smile and he bends over backwards to please her!'

—

It hadn't been so straightforward for Dhruv to pick up the pieces of his life. When he walked out of Anjolie's misshapen apartment that day, a gargantuan cloud hung over the sky and sank into his hammering heart. He couldn't breathe. He lit a cigarette and let the nicotine snatch his mind away. Cars darted past him as he walked and a big green bus stopped right in front of him. He left his car on the street outside her flat and got into the bus. He found a place by the window and sat down. Now he was higher. Now he was looking down at the city below. He stared out of the window as trees brushed by, bus stops raced past and people were whisked away. Brightly coloured posters of Tamil films were splashed on compound walls, all featuring a man and a woman in love.

He had a hole in his heart. It was as if someone had taken a surgical knife and severed off two inches of his heart. Now the rest of him was shrinking to fill the void.

A fat lady in an electric-blue sari and fake diamonds drooping from one side of her fleshy nose climbed in and sat next to him. She opened a stainless steel tiffin box and ate a dosa generously sprinkled with chilli powder. A lanky college boy stood in the aisle gaping at him with ill-fated jaws. A little girl of about seven or eight stood next to him sucking a bright orange lollipop. The bus stank of sweat and misfortune but it was soothing to be among strangers and mourn his loss anonymously. Soon he would have to go back to Tulsi and pretend, pretend that all was well, and then keep on pretending the day after and the day after that.

The conductor elbowed his way through the standing crowd and asked him which stop he was getting down at. The last one, he said and placed a twenty-rupee note in his hand. Broadway, the conductor said and handed him his change and the ticket. It flew out of the window as soon as it touched his hand. I just threw away my Broadway ticket, he thought mirthlessly.

He got off at Broadway and lit another cigarette. The pale orange sun was sinking and the approaching darkness saddened him further. He decided to go back home and face the music. I can't hide from the world forever, he thought, and waved down an auto-rickshaw. He stepped in and said Cenotaph Road to the driver without haggling and then he remembered that his car was parked outside Anjolie's apartment. Greenways Road, he corrected himself and wished she lived in Ambattur or Avadi or somewhere so far away that he wouldn't have to drive past her flat again.

He would never see Anjolie again. She had been adamant about that. It'll kill me, she had said to him with dark eyes that waltzed before his. She was going to change her phone number. And how she had kissed him before he left! A hundred times all over his face as if by replicating that kiss again and again she could make a recollection for posterity. She was going to abort their baby and she didn't want him there when she did it. Please, she had said with tears running down her flushed cheeks; it's easier for me this way. It was all about what was easier for *her*, he thought. What about him?

Dhruv reached Greenways Road and gave the driver two hundred-rupee notes and walked to his car. Thanks saar, romba thanks, screamed the ecstatic driver and Dhruv wished he were the driver.

His mint-white car stood spotlessly in the late evening street. He got into it and drove off. A sad old tune played and replayed in his head from a Malayalam film that he had seen with his mother when his parents had just broken up. He tried to visualize Anjolie's face as he had last seen it from her doorstep, but it disintegrated before his eyes: her succulent lips crumbled up, the outline of her jaw dimmed at the edges, the eyelashes stood up with a mind of their own and her eyes melted into oblivion.

He reached his flat in five minutes and parked the car. He dragged his feet to the staircase and every step resonated against his shoes. He slid the key into the keyhole and opened the door as the doorknob reflected his distorted face. He shut it softly and walked inside. He took off his shoes, he took off his skin-coloured socks and put one inside each shoe. He imagined the other skin-coloured socks sitting wordlessly in the closet and realized it took only two to make a matching pair.

He walked into the bedroom. Tulsi lay naked on the bed with tears in her eyes, her clothes lay abandoned on the floor. The room smelt of citronella and rose petals.

'I thought you'd never come back,' she said and hugged him tight.

'Don't be silly, Tuls. Where would I go?'

She kissed him and fondled his hair and lay on his shoulder caressing his neck. She told him it was all going to be fine, that they would adopt a baby girl and their lives would change. And she was right, it changed the moment he saw his little girl's face and her big black eyes. The hole in his heart filled and he expanded and became whole again.

15

I am holding a little jewellery box in my hand. It is studded with precious stones and when it is lit up by my bedside lamp at night, it resonates with memories. The two rubies are deep red and the large sapphire in the centre looks like the sky and the little yellow topazes in the corners glow in the dark like fireflies.

Sid gave it to me on our recent expedition to Jaisalmer. Our bones were creaking from the camel safari and we were lying in the desert sand staring at the sky when he pulled it out of his pocket and slid it into my hands quixotically. I thought he was offering me a ring and I jumped up and opened the box. It is made of precious stones, he said, and I admired the box under the setting sun, pretending I knew all along that there was no ring inside.

But on the last day of our trip, he kissed me passionately in the moving train and whispered that I was his princess as palaces whizzed past like stars in the distance. I look at it now, an empty promise on the bedside table, and wonder what made him give me this extravagant jewellery box that is the perfect size for a ring.

I settle down in bed, open *A Brave New World* and enter the fertilization room where ripened eggs are swimming in test tubes only to bud, proliferate, divide and grow into ninety-six identical twins each. Being a gynaecologist who refuses to create babies from test tubes, I am horrified at the thought. I think about the desperate need in human beings to procreate, the willingness of women to undergo the long emotionally, physically and financially draining process of IVF just because of some notional idea of biological.

My mind races back to the brave new world in my hands. Everyone belongs to everyone else, I repeat to myself, both intrigued and fascinated by the idea. But in this world of ours, the older, cowardly one, we sit around creating social formulae like marriage which state that everyone *doesn't* belong to everyone else and if we were to stray from that order we would be labelled as outlaws.

I think about Jean Paul Sartre and Simone de Beauvoir who had a relationship that was based not on fidelity but on honesty. They could have relationships with other people but they had made a pact to tell each other everything, to be scrupulously honest, especially about their writing. They knew that sexual passion ultimately comes to an end and they didn't want to tie each other down with commitment. They didn't want their relationship to become a routine. It was to be a free choice, continually renewed. They never lived together and many of their conversations took place in cafés and restaurants, over a meal, wine or whiskey. The cafés in Saint-Germain-des-Prés like Le Café de Flore and Les Deux Magots are legendary because the story goes that

Sartre and Beauvoir went there to keep warm in the brutally cold winters of the Occupation. They lived in cheap, unheated hotels, writing all day, and went to the cafés in the evening to huddle near the stove.

That is how I picture Sid and me, years later, huddled together to keep warm like we did by the bonfire in the desert before he gave me the little jewellery box.

It is time to go to bed. I have surgery scheduled at six in the morning but I can't put the book down even though it is way past midnight. I finally turn off the lamp and the jewellery box disappears with my room and I feel like Lenina, entitled to a complete and absolute holiday from reality. I picture swallowing six tablets of *soma*, and within a few minutes embark for lunar eternity.

———

The woman in the burqa got out of a Volkswagen Jetta and entered the Landmark basement on Nungambakkam High Road. She walked like she had walked in high heels all her life. The entrance door was to the right and the exit door to the left and on the wall in front of her between the two doors were two dozen posters of plays, dances and concerts in the city. She looked at them for a moment and then opened the door on the right and walked into the cool air-conditioned interiors. She breathed in the smell of new books that she loved so much and smiled to herself.

She lifted her veil. She was a lovely looking woman but she was terribly overweight. She was thankful for her black burqa because it cropped a few inches from her body. She ate more now that they were prosperous but she also read more. Now her library held more than just one book.

She had a collection of five hundred books which she had carefully arranged in alphabetical order.

It was five years since she stumbled upon the idea to make her husband's shop in Triplicane go online. Now he sold fancy lehenga-cholis and salwar-kameezes to Muslim brides worldwide. Now they lived in a beautiful house on Khader Nawaz Khan Road but she still visited her old neighbour in her Triplicane flat. She usually took a brand new DVD that they could tear open and watch.

Zubeida was a happy woman. She had a maid to do the dishes and a cook to make all that fare. Her oldest son Nabil was a teenager now and quite a gentleman. Everything had changed since the day she saw them walking home from school like poor little elves.

She looked around the bookshop. She wanted to buy a book called *Dear Scott, Dearest Zelda*. It was a collection of love letters between Zelda and Scott Fitzgerald. She had read *The Great Gatsby*, *This Side of Paradise* and *Tender Is the Night*. She had loved the story of the rise and fall of the promising young psychoanalyst and his wife Nicole, who was one of his patients. She had read that the novel was autobiographical and that the character of Nicole was based on Fitzgerald's glamorous wife Zelda. She was sure they didn't stock the book. She would have to ask them to order it for her, she thought and walked towards the Classics section. She was at W. There was Edgar Wallace, Horace Walpole, Albert Webster, H.G. Wells, Oscar Wilde, Virginia Woolf. She stopped.

She had almost bumped into a handsome young man who was looking at the exact same book. It was *Mrs Dalloway*. He smiled at her curiously, he had not seen many burqa-clad women browsing books. What beautiful, innocent eyes she had, the black kohl bringing out the brownness of her eyes under the white lights of the shop. Her plump hands looked much older than her face, they looked like they had made a thousand kilos of mutton biryani and yet they looked like they loved turning the pages of a book.

Zubeida studied him. He had faint lines around his eyes as though he was examining something. He was clean shaven, his jet-black hair was gelled back and matched the colour of his Lacoste polo shirt. He looked like he had just stepped out of the shower.

'There must be another *Mrs Dalloway* around,' he said and gave her the book.

'There must,' she said, 'but it'll probably be from a different publisher and have a different cover.'

'I like *this* Mrs Dalloway. I think she's rather beautiful and well-covered.'

Zubeida coughed. She hadn't spoken to another man in years.

'You keep this,' she said, thrusting the book at him and walking away. She walked through the shop, past the cash counter, out of the exit door and ran up the stairs. All these years she had felt like a rat in a trap in a room in a house waiting to be set free on a street somewhere and then the trap had expanded and filled the room and the room had expanded and filled the house and the house had expanded and filled the city. When she flew to Dubai recently for the shopping festival, the city had expanded and filled the whole wide world. But then, she thought, lowering the veil of her burqa over her face, she still felt like a rat in a trap. The world was the trap.

The man in the black polo shirt held *Mrs Dalloway* in his hands as though it was made of crystal and walked to the cash counter. When he pulled out his wallet from his jeans pocket, his business card slipped out and fell on the floor. He paid quickly and left. She was gone. He scolded himself for being so foolish. She looks old enough to be married with three kids, he said to himself. And yet she was his age and he wasn't even married yet. Once he was in his car, he pulled out *Mrs Dalloway* from the plastic bag and smiled at the cover.

'That man in the black shirt dropped his visiting card,' said someone at the counter and handed it over to the cashier.

Zubeida was right behind. She had come back because she had forgotten to place an order for *Dear Scott, Dearest Zelda*. She placed the order, picked up two classics and walked to the cash counter to pay. She looked at the card that lay abandoned on the counter.

Sandeep Bharadwaj, it said. *Landscape Architect.*

———

Megha had a dream.

She dreamt that she was wearing pants. And underneath the pants is a fairly long tail that is difficult to hide. She is in a room full of men and they are talking to her as if she has important things to say. They are shaking her hand and asking her about politics. 'What do you think of the parliament's provisions as to disqualification on grounds of defection?' a young gentleman asks her. Suddenly she realizes that she has an answer, she knows everything. She is about to tell him what she thinks when her tail peeps out of her pants and she runs out of the room.

Megha had another girl. Her fourth daughter was the luckiest. She was born with a broken heart. Her little heart had a combination of defects that made the left ventricle too small to pump blood. And because they were all moping over the birth of another baby girl, they took her to the surgeon too late and she was scarred for life. When she finally came out of the hospital and into her home, quivering and crippled for the rest of her life, her daddy lifted her up with tears in his eyes and kissed her.

Everybody fell in love with her sad little face and motionless eyes: the gigantic duck that waddled around her cradle, the egg-faced creature with skinny arms and skinny legs, and the rest of the animal farm. And after her birth, girls were equal to boys in the straggling white mansion in Purasawalkam.

———

Had you seen her from a rickshaw over the Anna Flyover, she would have looked like a white rabbit. Had you seen her from the other side of Mount Road where gigantesque billboards of Tamil films towered over gulmohar trees, had you seen the bounce of her quick steps towards Greams Road, you would have thought she was a young girl. But if you were passing her on the pavement, you would have known that she was fifty.

When most working people were preparing to retire, she started to work. In fact, she had started working that day itself and she was going over every moment of the day in her head, from the instant she entered the blue and yellow interiors of the travel agency where she sat in front of a computer with the world at her fingertips, to the present when she walked carelessly on the pavement like a schoolgirl.

She still couldn't believe they had chosen her over all the young girls who had turned up for the interview. And considering she had stopped working over twenty years ago, she had expected a rejection letter. Instead, they had called her a few hours after the interview to tell her she was hired. She didn't need the money but she *needed* to work.

When she was about to go back to the airlines after her maternity leave, her toddler turned around on the first day of school and asked her if she would be there when she came back home. Yes, she had said, looking into those worried brown eyes, and gave up the idea of working forever. But now her toddler was twenty-five. And she was in LA. Why hasn't she called me yet? Could she have forgotten my fiftieth birthday? After all, a fiftieth birthday was momentous, wasn't it?

She walked into Greams Lane. She walked past a few houses and opened the gate. Her husband's car was not there. He must have gone to play tennis, she thought and opened the door. The windows were open and she made a little note in her head to tell her husband to shut them when he went out. The house looks unusually clean, she thought as she stepped inside. I wonder what *he's* been up to.

She stepped into the shower. As the cool water fell on her face and her hair became wetter and heavier, she thought about Pooja once again. When she was a little girl, she played with the soap while her mother showered, blowing on the soap till bubbles burst forth. Suddenly she had the urge to make gulab jamuns. She towelled herself dry and slipped into a nightgown and went to the kitchen. She tore open a packet of Carnation milk powder and poured it into a bowl. She added some milk and butter and began kneading the dough. She divided the dough into little pieces and counted them. There were at least fifty of them. Her husband was diabetic. Then why am I making so many, she wondered. But she made them anyway and as she rolled the dough into smooth little balls in the palm of her hands, she began to relax. She slipped the balls into hot oil from the side of the pan and they sank to the bottom. She shook the pan ever so gently to keep the balls from browning on one side and hummed a tune. The balls rose to the surface and she dropped them into sugar syrup. She placed the hot bowl of jamuns under the fan and tried Pooja one more time. The phone rang and rang. It was six in the morning in LA; why wasn't her daughter home?

She put one big jamun into her mouth. Its sweetness entered her body and she felt warm and safe. But where was her husband? And where was her daughter? Was she at an early morning shoot? Or was she not back from last night's shoot? She had said something about a shoot on Sunset Boulevard for an experimental film that she was making. She began to worry. She tried her mobile.

And then the doorbell rang. It must be her husband getting back from tennis. She put the phone down and opened the door. A lovely young woman stood outside with an enormous suitcase. She took one look at her and burst into tears. The woman with the suitcase took her into her arms.

'Happy Birthday, mama,' said Pooja and kissed her tears away.

———

If this hadn't been the story of these six women, it would have been ours, you and me walking through the sunset in the Andamans the year before the Tsunami came. You looking at the wayward clouds and me looking at you in joy. It would have been about the time we flew back in the turbulent Indian Airlines aircraft from the Maldives, holding hands while the sun coloured the sky and then letting go at the airport where you took a flight out of India, out of my life. I came home that night with a hollow feeling in my bones, as if they were made of air, as if they might fly away if I let go and leave my sinking heart behind. It would have been about our last breakfast at Flurys when I came to see you in Calcutta; you were writing that endless article for the *Lonely Planet* and the restaurant was filled with Easter eggs in all sizes, colours and flavours but in that one unalterable shape that reminded me of you for ages. It would have been about that dark red night when we polished off a bottle of Red Riband vodka, looked through the sparkling clean bottle and imagined sitting in some quaint little airport looking at flight departures and choosing where to go. But it was a miserably hot night even for Madras, and you were leaving the next day.

But darling, in all my memories of you, it's sunshine, it's rain, it's an aquamarine holiday; it's the sky peeping down to touch my face like the soft blue blanket that covered me when I was little. And do you know what it tells me? It tells me that it is not real. It was never real. It was always a holiday, a holiday of two minds that never met in real time.

Now it's dark. Aside from the red balloons that catch the light around their egg-like exteriors, it's mostly dark. It's New Year's Eve. Ten years have gone by in the new millennium, and it's not so new now. I am at a gathering in a beach resort, one of the several little retreats scattered along the shore in Mahaballipuram. There are red balloons everywhere: on the walls, on the windows and on the false ceiling of the little seafood restaurant by the sea. We are sitting outside drinking champagne, an oddity in these parts of the world. I wonder what I am celebrating. A new year? A new life?

There is a conversation going on at the table, pillow talk on the chairs, laughter at the edges, but I can only hear the sea, I can only see the waves rising and falling and beating against the sand. I always thought that somewhere beyond the sea, somewhere waiting for me, my lover stands on golden sand and watches the ships go by.

That's how I imagined Sid, like a Frank Sinatra song, standing at the edge of the sand, his feet tucked in the water, looking at the ships that sail past. But I was wrong. He was looking at a woman who went sailing – a blond Norwegian windsurfer to be precise.

And what's wrong with that? I never expected Sid to be faithful to me. How can I when I don't believe in the idea of tying somebody down with rules? So what if he looked at a woman who went sailing?

You're my soul mate, he said on the phone this morning, and nothing is going to change that. Don't you marry your soul mate, I wanted to ask but I knew the answer. A soul mate is just a mating of souls, like animals. If he had asked me to marry him, I would have said yes long ago. But he never asked, and I went on pretending that I was not the marrying type. I pretended for years and years until I believed my own lies. Did he believe them too? Is that why he never asked?

It would be lovely to suppose that, but let's not fool ourselves. Sid never asked because he never felt it. Besides, he is a free spirit, a traveller with no frontiers, and I am a doctor who has her frontiers clearly marked, etched around five-and-a-half grounds in Mylapore.

Then what made him ask *her*?

When I think of the pain Dhruv and Anjolie must have felt, I envy them. They parted so dramatically, but mostly I envy them because when you separate after falling into each other's arms day after day, it comes as a shock to the senses, and you wallow in pain, you wallow in so much pain that the border between pain and pleasure slowly fades away, until one day you wake up and you are whole again.

I never saw Sid every day. Our moments together were few and far between. I lived with the idea of seeing him every day, I lived with the idea of love, and ideas are hard to wipe away. I always thought it would end like a fairytale. I would be Cinderella in the last act and he would be my prince, my champion, my saviour. But who was I kidding? I was no princess, I was just wearing a costume, and when he kissed me I turned into a frog.

I never told him how much I loved him because I was waiting for him to tell me. Because a man tells a woman first. And so, for all my preaching that women can do anything that men can do, I failed miserably to believe myself, at least in this one little area called love. And isn't love what makes the world go round? No, says a voice in my head. The world was born spinning and, like a figure skater centred on a single point on the ice, it keeps on spinning.

I look at the sky. Stars are strewn like sawdust on the floor and a pale jaundiced moon lies in a corner inconspicuously. I can't wait for the night to end. I can't wait to go home. I hear fireworks. The sky sprinkles golden flowers like the fountain in grandfather's house that was switched on for special occasions. People around me are making calls. I close my ears and look at the sea.

I can't help but wonder, what if? What if I had left Madras when it was still called Madras and followed Sid around the world when he had asked me to? Would we be together today?

My mobile rings. The clinic is calling to tell me that the woman in 212 has gone into labour. I am happy to leave this place, happy to stop pretending that all is well with the world. I don't know what is worse, the miserable feeling or pretending that there's no miserable feeling. I drive the long stretch towards the city in silence. I reach the clinic, deliver a brand new baby and go to the consultation room. I sit at my desk and watch the pale yellow curtains standing still in time. I drink coffee. I write. I drink more coffee.

In the case of a roulette wheel, if the force of the hand and the period of that force are known, the number on which the ball stops would be a certainty. But in life we never know that force. All we see is the number on which the ball has stopped. Half of them are even, and half of them are terribly odd.

It is clearer now. The examination table lights up, the dates on the calendar begin to glow and the Doppler comes alive. I draw the curtains and watch the sun climb the jagged Chennai skyline like a baby into her mother's lap. There is a knock on the door, the first patient is here. And then they come in one after the other like ants into a honey jar. They spread their legs and look at me with hope and I wish, how I wish I could give them wings to fly.

Acknowledgements

I would like to thank my publisher, V.K. Karthika, for reading that first foggy purple line and getting back in three days to say yes and then for her precious suggestions that followed. Neelini Sarkar, my editor, for her delightfully prompt and meticulous pointers that took it to the next level. Prema Raghunath, for rapturously reading the embryonic manuscript. Dr Uma Ram, for being the wonderful gynaecologist that she is, and for generously giving her time to go over the manuscript with me. Dr Sheela Nambiar, for her fresh insight into her profession. Tishani Doshi, for being there when one writer needs another.

And then the men in my life. My dad, for giving me the incredible gift of writing. My very own Santa Claus, Praveen, for sustaining me page after page. Kumaravel, for that unforgettable ride in the flying trains that made me see Madras with new eyes. Avinash, for thinking that I was going to win the Booker when I wrote chapter one.

Lastly, this book wouldn't have been written if I hadn't read *The New Our Bodies, Ourselves* by the Boston Women's Health Book Collective, which helped me not only to demystify medicine but women themselves, and taught me how important it is for women to 'claim' their bodies by taking charge of their reproduction and possess the power to change their lives.